VAMPIRES
I HAVE KISSED

14 TALES OF BLOODCURDLING ROMANCE

LYDIA GALT

SWEETWATER
PRESS

SWEETWATER
PRESS

Vampires I Have Kissed

Copyright © 2007 Cliff Road Books, Inc.
Produced by arrangement with Sweetwater Press

ISBN-13: 978-1-58173-670-0
ISBN-10: 1-58173-670-3

Cover design by Pat Covert

VAMPIRES
I HAVE KISSED

TABLE OF CONTENTS

PARIS, 1874

Colette wrapped a heavy wool shawl around her shoulders and shut the door quietly behind her as she stepped into the chilly morning air. Her father was ill upstairs, and she wanted to get out and finish the shopping before he awoke. In her mind, she ran through the list of what she needed—bread, strawberries, jam, cheese, and wine. All around her, Paris was waking up for the day. Flower merchants were misting and arranging their buckets of blooms, and the street sweepers worked quickly to clean up the grime and debris of the previous evening.

As she approached the bakery, Colette inhaled the delicious scent of freshly baked bread. Although it was hard to rise as early as she did, it was worth it, to be among the first customers walking home with a perfect, still-warm baguette.

Colette bought her bread and placed it in the basket she carried. She was fumbling to put several coins back into her change purse when she tripped over the outstretched leg of a vagrant propped against the wall of a building.

"Oh, excuse me," Colette cried, startled. "I didn't see

you there." Her words might have been wasted, for the man appeared to be sleeping. But then he opened one eye, startling in its dark color, and he spoke.

"It is nothing, do not worry, mademoiselle," the vagrant mumbled. He closed his eye again and went back to resting. Colette wanted to move along and continue her errands, but she felt her body arrested by the strangeness of the man's eye. She was drawn to him, curious and afraid, all at once.

"Sir," she offered, "is there anything I can do for you? Can I give you a few centimes, perhaps?" Even as she spoke them, the words surprised her. Colette was a cautious person, and she rarely spoke to strange men. She had certainly never tried to start a conversation by offering money to a sleeping vagrant. But for some reason, she couldn't help herself.

The man opened his eyes and stared at her. She was held in place by the intensity of his gaze. She had never seen eyes so dark before—nearly black to the edges, and she was startled by their almost animal quality.

"There is nothing you can do for me." He sounded like a man without hope. "Please, just go on. There is nothing anyone can do."

Colette came back to her senses and walked on. But she was so shaken by the whole business of the man on the street that she forgot to buy jam or cheese and walked automatically back toward home. "Oh well," she thought distractedly, "Father and I will just have to make do with butter on our bread today."

—

That night, Colette's dreams were disturbed. She dreamed of the man's eyes, staring at her with oppressive force and heat. When she awoke the next morning, she had kicked the thin cover from her bed onto the floor.

Before she left the house, she wrapped up a slice of chocolate cake in paper and put it in her basket. She did not know if she'd ever see him again, but somewhere deep inside herself, she hoped.

Her hope turned out to be well-founded. As she neared the bakery, there was the man resting in same spot and position that he'd been in the day before. Colette forgot about wanting to be first in line to buy a baguette, and kneeled down beside him. She placed her hand on his arm. His clothes were stiff with dirt and sweat, but rather than bothering Colette, this only made her feel a surge of sympathy for him.

"Sir, excuse me. I have brought you something." The man looked up with a surprised expression, and Colette wondered how long it had been since anyone had called him "sir."

He nodded, seeming to recognize her. She presented him with the cake, and as he stared at it, his eyes filled with tears.

"You are too kind, mademoiselle. What have I done to deserve such a gift?" To Colette's surprise, he did not begin to eat the cake, but just held it in his hands.

"Why, I just thought that you must be hungry. Please, eat." She tried to help him unwrap the cake, but he stopped her, taking her hands in his.

"You do not understand. I have done nothing to

deserve this; it's just the opposite. I will not eat this cake, and even if I did, it would do nothing to nourish me. I am one of the damned, mademoiselle. Thank you for your kindness, but you must leave me be." The look in his eyes had changed quickly from gratitude to something near anger. Colette became frightened. Without another word, she left the cake sitting on the ground near the man and hurried away.

—

Despite his urgings, Colette could not get him out of her thoughts. This was in part because of her kind nature; she'd always been one to leave food out for stray animals, or volunteer to nurse a sick relative. But her feelings for the man did not spring from charity alone. She felt haunted by him. She had a singular need to help him, or if she could not help, to simply be near him in his suffering.

She returned to the spot the next day with a new approach. "Now you listen to me," she said sternly, once she had stomped on the ground next to the man to awaken him.

He looked up. "Yes?"

Colette found that she wasn't quite sure what to demand of him. He owed her nothing, and yet, she felt that in a way, he did. "I want to know about you. I want to know why you must be so stubborn, to refuse any help. You are too thin, and probably ill. Do you want to die?"

To her surprise, he began to laugh. It was the first time she'd seen even a hint of a smile on his face. "That, my lady, is exactly what I want. And yet for some reason, you seem determined to interfere. Why should it trouble you, the death of a vagrant, a good-for-nothing, a man you do not even know?"

She didn't have a good answer. "Well, certainly you are more that that, or used to be at some time. What is your name? You must have a name."

"My name is Frederic."

Colette extended her hand. "And mine is Colette." They shook hands. "There," Colette said. "Now we know each other."

Frederic reluctantly agreed to go to a café with Colette for a cup of coffee, but once they were there, he refused to drink anything. Colette knew that he was only humoring her so that she would stop bothering him, but she decided that she would use the time to convince him to accept some help. He sat in silence, staring at Colette from across the table as she drank her coffee.

"Frederic," she began, "we are all God's creatures. Why would you say that you are one of the damned? What could you have done so terrible that you no longer want to live?"

"It is no mere mortal sin. My very flesh is changed. I am no longer one of God's creatures. You would not understand."

Colette was bewildered, so she said nothing. Frederic went on. "I gain my life at the expense of others."

Colette inhaled sharply. "A murderer?" she asked. Her head was swarmed with dizziness and fear. Perhaps she had gotten herself into a dangerous situation, and should have heeded her father's advice never to speak to strange men.

"A murderer, perhaps, but not by choice."

"Well, if not by choice, then how?"

Frederic leaned in close to her over the table and whispered. "A vampire, Colette. To live, I must feed. I must drink the blood of human beings. And if my victims do not die themselves, they face a fate worse than death. They become like me, one of the damned."

Frederic leaned back in his seat and heaved a great, sad sigh. "So now you know. Now you understand why I, myself, must cease to live."

Colette was stunned. Acting on instinct, unable to control her own movements, she rose and ran from the café.

—

It took several days for Colette to recover from the shock of what she'd heard at the café. She stayed in bed for most of the time, doing only the bare minimum in her duties caring for her father. The rest of the time, she lay on her back, thinking.

Despite what all her senses told her—that she should forget Frederic and never try to see him again—something inside her told her that was impossible. She was pulled toward him, her heart and her thoughts, all of the time. On the third day, she made her fateful decision.

As she left her home for the final time, she kissed her sleeping father on his cheek and said a tearful prayer over him. Then she called on her cousin across town, saying that she had to leave Paris for a while, and getting her cousin's promise to take care of the old man while she was away. She walked down to where she knew Frederic would be sitting and found him, closer to death than she had ever seen anyone before. He was pale and thin, his head resting weakly against the wall behind him.

Colette kneeled down in a panic. "Frederic! Frederic, please, wake up. I've come for you. I want to be with you, like you, one of your kind."

He shook his head weakly, barely able to move. "No. I could never take you. I could never make you into what I am, a monster."

"If you are damned, then I am damned, too. Please. Take me. Let me save you. Would it not make life bearable, to have someone by your side? Someone to go through all of this with you?"

He shook his head again, but Colette took his face in her hands, and pressed it to her neck.

Like a wild animal, something in Frederic awoke, and against his will, he bit. He was so hungry, so close to death, and when his teeth sunk into Colette, he felt his life force returning. Her blood coursed into him. He was alive again, in a way, and the two of them were together. They would always be.

THE BAR

Walking down the dark sidewalk toward his favorite bar, John Rayburn shrugged his shoulders against the cold and pulled his jacket tighter around himself. It was late, and the street was nearly deserted. John walked on with determination, anxious to get to the bar. He looked forward to wrapping his hand around a warm tumbler of bourbon, feeling the burning liquid slide down his throat. Even more than that, he looked forward to seeing her.

As John opened the door to Edgar's, a drift of heavy smoke floated out into the frozen night. Edgar's was a dimly lit bar frequented mostly by middle-aged regulars who simply wanted a warm place to drink, somewhere that they wouldn't be bothered by dance music or unwanted small talk. Drunks, John thought as he looked around the room at the clientele. Like me.

He walked up to the bar. Edgar nodded a hello and slid John a bourbon and a beer, no questions asked. John came here often enough that he rarely had to give his order to the bartender.

Some of John's buddies called to him from the pool table as he walked to a small table in the corner of the room. "Hey John! How about a game?" John shook his head. Although he was good at pool, probably the best player at the bar, he hadn't felt like playing lately. His friends had noticed it, and they'd started giving him a hard time about it. "Oh, sure," one of them called as he racked the balls on the table. "You just sit right there and keep staring. Maybe tonight she'll talk to you." The others laughed drunkenly, but it didn't bother John.

A few minutes later, she walked in. To John, she was like a bright candle entering the dark room. She shed her heavy coat and scarf, shaking out her long, dark curls. She was a not a conventionally good-looking woman. She had a large sturdy shape, and her facial features were too heavy and pronounced to ever be called pretty. But there was something about her that drew John to her. He didn't want to stop looking at her, as if her face was some kind of mystery that only he could figure out.

John had been watching her for about a month, ever since she'd started bartending at Edgar's. He had overheard that her name was Helen, but he'd never had the courage to speak to her directly. She made him feel so shy that he nearly always turned away when she returned his stare.

But tonight was different. Maybe it was that he'd been drinking even before he got to the bar, but John that night, felt courageous. As Helen swiped a wet rag over the bar, John stared at her. When she caught his eye, he walked over to her.

"I'm John," he said, holding out his hand. She took it. Her hand was smooth and cold, like a stone worn by the water.

"I know who you are. I'm Helen."

"Yes, I know."

There was an instant attraction between them. John felt like there were sparks of electricity charging the air around him.

"Say, Helen, what would you say about having a drink with me?"

She smiled coyly. "John, I'm on duty."

"Well, how about after?"

"I don't get off until about three o'clock," Helen said.

John shrugged. "That's okay. I'm a night owl myself."

Helen closed her eyes and smiled. "I can't tell you how glad I am to hear that."

Hmm, that's an odd thing to say, John thought. He shrugged it off though, just glad to have made a date with Helen.

The night seemed to drag on. John wished each minute away, eager for the time when he would sit down alone with Helen. The customers eventually began to pay their tabs and stumble out of the bar. When everyone was gone, Helen let John sweep the floor while she washed glasses and restocked the bar. As they worked, there was easy conversation between them. John felt as if he'd known Helen for a long time. They didn't talk much about their pasts; mostly, they talked about things that went on at the bar—people they knew in common, and things like that.

When they were done cleaning, John looked at his watch. Four-thirty. He should be tired by now, but he wasn't. Talking with Helen made him feel young and full of energy. "Say, Helen," he proposed, "I know it's late, but would you let me buy you some breakfast?"

Helen looked at her own watch, and then out of the bar's one small window. "Oh, my goodness. I didn't realize how early it had gotten!" She sounded nervous. "I've really enjoyed talking to you, John. I lost track of time. I have to be going. Come on now," she said as she shooed him out of the bar and locked the door behind them.

John was confused. He planted a kiss on Helen's cheek. "Can I see you again?" he asked lamely.

"Of course. Come back tomorrow," she said over her shoulder, already walking away from him at a fast pace.

John showed up again the next night, a Sunday. He'd looked forward to seeing Helen all day, and he was glad that the bar wasn't very crowded so that he could talk to her as she worked. They closed up earlier than usual. Helen asked John to stick around again.

The two of them sat down at a small table, John with his bourbon and Helen with a glass of wine. Under the hanging light, John noticed again how beautiful Helen was. She looked to be about forty years old, but her skin showed no signs of wrinkling or age. She had the skin of a young girl, but her eyes were wise, and seemed very old.

"So, Helen, you've never told me much about your life before now. Where are you from? What did you do before you came to work at Edgar's?"

She hesitated. "Oh, John. The past is past, right? I'd much prefer to think about now. Wouldn't you?"

As curious as he was about Helen, there were many things about John's own past that he would just as soon forget. He decided that she had that right, too, and he didn't press her.

"Okay. Agreed."

"Good." Helen laid her hand on top of John's. A thrill shot through him. He felt the heat running up his arm, warming his face and then his stomach. He leaned in toward her.

"Helen," he whispered into her ear.

"Yes," she breathed. Her breath was sweet as it rushed across John's cheek. Her hair fell around his face like a heavy curtain.

"I want to be with you." John felt silly as soon as he said it. The words had just come out of him; he wasn't exactly sure what he meant, but thought that they sounded trite and juvenile, and didn't do justice to the deep feelings that he was having.

But Helen didn't seem to mind. "I know you do." She turned her face upward to kiss him. John felt his breath quickening and the blood pulsing through him as his mouth pressed against Helen's. The kiss lingered, and then she pulled away.

"You said that you wanted to be with me. I think that's true. I think," she said with a devilish smile, "that you might want to be with me for a very long time. Forever even."

John nodded. He felt intoxicated, not just by the bourbon but also by Helen's kiss and her words. He wasn't sure what was going on, and he didn't really care. Was Helen asking him to marry her?

"John, what if you could forget your past? What if you could have everything to look forward to? A hundred lifetimes. An infinite string of nights to come, all of them yours, all of them ours, together."

Helen's words sounded like poetry to John. Beautiful, but incomprehensible. "I'm afraid I don't follow."

"You don't have to understand. Just trust me. Will you trust me?"

John nodded. He would do anything for her. They leaned in towards each other. Just before Helen's parted lips reached his, John saw a shard of light glinting off of her teeth. The kiss that followed made John feel like his head was spinning. He had never felt this way before. Helen brought her hands to John's cheeks and turned his head to the side. She buried her face in the crook of his neck. John held her close as she took several deep, hungry breaths.

And then he felt the sting as she plunged her teeth into the soft flesh of his neck.

John tried to yell but couldn't make a sound. Helen held her mouth in place, drinking from him, pulling the life from his veins. As the blood rushed from him, John felt himself getting weaker and weaker.

What was happening? Was he dying? John considered the possibility, but somehow it didn't bother him. Helen's bite was painful, but it was also the most thrilling thing he'd ever felt. As he got weaker, he imagined that he was giving himself, body and soul, over to this beautiful woman.

It finally stopped. Helen withdrew, and just before John passed out on the table, he saw her drawing a cocktail napkin across her bloody mouth.

—

John awoke feeling heavy, as if he'd been asleep for days. He'd dreamed of a blackness so deep that he'd thought he might never wake up from it.

Helen was shaking his shoulder bringing him back to consciousness. "Come on. Get up. We need to get home."

Home? John thought. He still felt unbelievably weak, and he wanted to stay there sleeping with his head on the table. "No," he groaned. "Let me sleep."

"Trust me. That's not a good idea. It will be morning soon, and you won't enjoy the sunlight." Helen said. She leaned over and kissed his neck, letting her tongue slide slowly across the open wound where she'd bitten him.

John got up and stretched. His limbs felt like lead as he followed Helen out of the bar.

"Where are we going?"

"Home. We're going home." John nodded, remembering the night before, and beginning to understand. He was with Helen now. Forever. Whatever she was, he was too. John didn't know what his new life would have in store for him, but as he walked through the night, he left the past behind him in each footstep. He would follow Helen wherever she led, into an endless string of nighttimes.

DENISE'S DEBUT

"Denise, honey, remember you have your final fitting after school today. Three thirty. Don't be late, alright?" Denise Lewis rolled her eyes. For the past three weeks, her mother had been hounding her with reminders and instructions for her "coming out" at the Bathory Society's annual debutante ball. It was a tradition among all the girls in her family's social circle, the wealthy, old-money elite of the town of Bellingview.

"Alright, Mom! I won't forget. Stop pestering me!" Denise had not even wanted to participate in the ball to begin with. To her, it seemed like a dated, pretentious custom. She'd been allowed to go on dates for two years already, so the idea of being "presented to suitors in society" seemed redundant and silly.

But when she had confessed her hesitation at the dinner table one night, her parents nearly had a fit. Her mother got hysterical, close to tears, and her father had been angrier than she'd ever seen him. Jeez, she thought. She knew the Bathory Society was important to her father, with its monthly secret meetings and socials, but she'd never known how important it was to him that she join it as well on her eighteenth birthday. Even her older brother

Allen had been shocked that she didn't want to participate. So Denise gave in pretty quickly, and since then, her life had been a whirlwind of dress fittings, shoe shopping, and debutante luncheons. Ridiculous, she thought. At least it would all be over with by Saturday, and she could stop hearing about it.

There was another thing adding to Denise's reluctance about the upcoming ball. It was one of the Society's rules that each debutante had to be escorted by a male member. Denise had turned her nose up at all of her mother's suggestions for dates—they were mostly boys who attended the same private school that she did—longtime friends of the family, and Denise found them all rather snobby and boring. Finally, in a moment of weakness and frustration, she'd agreed to let her mother fix her up with a college boy who would be coming into town. Devon Hampton. Denise had never met him or even seen a picture of him, and she expected that he would just be a carbon copy of the other boys her mother had suggested. She was already making plans about how to ditch him once the bows and courtesies were over.

Denise had her keys in hand and was on the way out the door when her mother yelled after her.

"Oh, I almost forgot! Don't make plans for Friday night. The Hamptons are coming over for dinner."

"Jeez, Mom! I don't want to…"

"Oh come on, don't you want to get acquainted with your date? He's very handsome. I think you'll like him. And besides, I'm not asking here. I'm telling. Dinner, Friday night, seven o'clock."

"Fine," Denise yelled, closing the door with a little more force than she needed to.

—

Her first real shock of the week came that afternoon at the final dress fitting. Up until that point, she had been trying on sample dresses—dull pink, dirty lavender, sky blue—in colors no one would want to wear. The tailor assured her that the final dress would not be any of these colors, and Denise just assumed that like other debutante balls, the girls at the Bathory society would be wearing white. She was struck speechless when the tailor, a small, old woman, pulled her dress out of the plastic wrapping, and she saw that it was a deep crimson color.

"Red? Is this another sample dress?" Denise asked, her heart racing in panic. Her mother would absolutely kill her if she'd ordered the wrong dress. She could almost hear her shrill cries now. Red, at a debutante ball? What were you thinking? Heads would roll, Denise was sure.

"Yes, that's right dear. The Bathory Ball, isn't it?"

Denise nodded.

"Trust me, I have been tailoring dresses for this ball for years. All of the girls will be wearing this color. You will fit right in. Now try it on, dear."

Denise slipped out of her jeans and T-shirt and stepped into the massive pile of gorgeous red satin. She exhaled as the tailor zipped the tight bodice, and then she looked in the mirror.

She was transformed. The red fabric clung to her narrow waist and pooled luxuriously on the floor around her. Lace edging trimmed the strapless bodice and accentuated her long, pale neck.

"Beautiful," the tailor said. Denise had to agree.

—

On Friday, Denise got ready for dinner with the Hamptons. She was so excited about wearing the red dress that she didn't gripe or complain about the obligation. She even took a little extra time with her hair and applied some light perfume, on the off chance that Devon Hampton didn't turn out to be a total dud.

She was still upstairs getting ready when the doorbell rang. She heard the voices of everyone as they got reacquainted, and didn't go downstairs until her mother called up for her to do so.

The group exchanged their hellos and nice to meet yous. Denise was introduced to Mr. and Mrs. Hampton, an elegant-looking couple probably in their mid-fifties. And then, for the first time, she noticed Devon Hampton. At least, she assumed it was Devon Hampton. The young man standing in front of her was so beautiful that he could have been a romance-novel cover model, or even a hallucination. He had a fine, sculpted face and flawless skin. His lips were full and dark, and his eyes were light blue, almost wolf-like. The introduction was a blur for Denise, who could barely pull herself together enough to speak. She looked over at her mother, who was grinning a self-satisfied smile at Denise's reaction to the fix-up.

At dinner, Denise didn't eat much. Instead she pushed food around on her plate while sneaking discreet glances at Devon, who was always looking back at her. When the dessert plates were finally cleared away, Mrs. Lewis suggested that the two of them go sit for a while on the veranda.

Devon held the door open as Denise walked through it, into the star-flecked night. One of the nice things about living in Bellingview was its distance from the city lights. A person could look up and be startled by the stark contrast of silver stars against a black sky. Stargazing was one of Denise's favorite things to do at night, and judging by the rapturous look on his face as he stared upward, Devon shared this passion.

"I love it out here," Denise confided.

"It's breathtaking," said Devon.

"Can you see the stars like this where you go to school?"

He shook his head sadly. "Not hardly. The place is too built-up and commercialized. All the streetlights and neon make it look like daytime, even in the middle of the night."

He hesitated, but Denise could tell that he wanted to say more. Bravely, her heart pounding, she put her hand on top of his and squeezed his palm. He went on. "There's a place I like to go to escape, though. A little lake in the woods about twenty miles from campus. It's so quiet out there. On a clear night, the moon is so bright that you don't even need a flashlight. I have a little rowboat, and I take it out on the lake probably a couple of nights a week." Devon gave Denise a quick glance and a shy, embarrassed smile. "I've never told anyone about it before," he confessed.

Denise was flooded with tenderness toward this sensitive, beautiful man. She imagined him sneaking away from campus, perhaps telling his friends that he couldn't make the fraternity party because he had to study, when all he really wanted was to go and enjoy a beautiful, quiet night on the lake.

"That's wonderful, Devon. It's nothing to be embarrassed about! I'd love to go there with you sometime, if it would be alright with you." She didn't look into his eyes as she said the words, worried that she might sound too bold or pushy.

But Devon took her chin in his hand guided it toward him. He stared deep into her eyes. "I'd like that very much." He was smiling. Denise tried to lean in, thinking that he would kiss her, but Devon held her off. "No. Not yet. We have tomorrow to look forward to."

And Denise did look forward to it. The next day was Saturday, the day of the ball, and Denise was up with the sun. She hadn't been up that early on a weekend since she was a child, afraid of missing her favorite cartoons. When she heard her mother bustling around in the kitchen, she went downstairs to get a glass of milk, but was too nervous to eat. Mrs. Lewis smiled, gloating. "So, you are looking forward to the ball, at least a little?"

Denise was too happy to be annoyed by her mother's implied "I-told-you-so." "As a matter of fact, I am," she said, finishing the glass of milk, and then grabbing her keys and heading for the door. She was off to the drugstore, in search of a nail polish that would match the shade of her dress exactly.

—

At last, it was time to go to the club where the ball would be held. Denise packed up her dress, shoes, and jewelry, and hopped into the car with her mother.

"You're going to look amazing, honey." Mrs. Lewis gave her a smile so full of love and pride that Denise was truly glad she'd agreed to take part in the ball. And of course, it didn't hurt that she was about to put on that stunning red dress and be escorted across the stage by Devon Hampton.

Denise and Mrs. Lewis made their way to the dressing area in the back of the club. Half a dozen other girls were already there in various stages of frenzy and undress, some of them pulling body-shapers over their hips, others in robes, fixing their hair or makeup. They were all Denise's friends from school, and they greeted her with shrieks and giggles. Everyone seemed to be in high spirits. This night was going to be a lot of fun after all, thought Denise.

An hour later everyone was dressed and ready, and the ball coordinator came in to line the girls up to be presented. None of them had been allowed to see the ballroom yet; it was supposed to be a surprise. From the other room, music began playing. The coordinator tapped the first girl, Anne Marie Taylor, and she walked out onto the stage. The other girls, Denise included, huddled in the wings to watch what happened. Up until then, everything about the ball had been shrouded in secrecy. None of them really knew what to expect, and this was their first glimpse into what was happening. What they saw took Denise's breath away.

The room was decorated in a sea of red. Red roses, probably thousands of them, carpeted the floor and the buffet tables. Tiny white lights dotted the scene, twinkling like stars. Denise's stomach was growling from the missed meal, and she was surprised to notice that there was no food on the tables. In the middle of the stage was a tall stone basin similar to a birdbath. Denise couldn't imagine what it might be for. And yet the strangest part of the whole scene was the audience. Denise looked out at them, the faces of people that she'd known nearly her whole life, and she was barely able to recognize them. Their expressions were changed, twisted into a strange kind of hunger, and their eyes gleamed eagerly. The sight gave Denise a deep chill all the way down her spine.

Anne Marie stepped out onto the stage, walking toward her date. His face shared the expression of the other audience members, a crazed kind of hunger. All of the sudden, Denise was terrified. She grabbed the hands of the girls in front and behind her, and they squeezed.

When Anne Marie reached the center of the stage, her date wrapped his arms around her, buried his face in the crook of her neck, and bit deeply. The girl standing behind Denise swooned, as if to faint. The ball coordinator rushed over and steadied her. "Don't be afraid," she said. "This is all a part of it. Just enjoy it, don't be afraid."

On stage, Anne Marie's date stood over the stone basin and opened his mouth, releasing a stream of crimson blood into it. Anne Marie's seemed to have passed out. Her date picked her up and carried her the rest of the way down the stage. Panic reflected in the eyes of the girls backstage. What was happening to them?

The coordinator was there to stop them from running away. One by one, she sent them out onto the stage to meet their dates, until it was Denise's turn. On shaking legs, she walked toward Devon. When they met in the middle of the stage, he took her in his arms. It was only her strong emotion toward him that kept her from turning and running in the other direction when she saw that the stone basin was halfway filled with blood.

"Don't be afraid. I'm here with you," Devon whispered into Denise's ear. Then he put his warm lips on her neck and bit, sucking with gentle pressure. Denise felt herself go weak as the blood rushed out of her. She gave herself over entirely to Devon, who held her up as her legs went limp beneath her. Before she lost consciousness, she saw devilish grins on the faces of her parents in the crowd. The white lights swam around the rose-filled room, like little stars on a blood-red sea.

THE NEW GIRL

"Hey, Jim, have you gotten a look at the new girl?" Scott set his tray of pizza down on the lunch table and raised one eyebrow as he nodded in the direction of Maria Till. This was her first day at Ridgewood High, and she was sitting at a lunch table all by herself.

Jim felt his face turning red. The truth was that he had noticed Maria. Mr. Brubaker had made the new student introduce herself to his math class that morning. Jim had hardly been able to stop staring at her—her black hair shiny as glass, and the large dark eyes, rimmed with a thick fringe of lashes, which she kept downcast, staring at the floor. In fact, she was quite the opposite of Jim's "type." His last girlfriend had been a cheerleader—blond, tan, and athletic. Maria, on the other hand, was rail thin and deathly pale. In a way, she almost looked ill. But Jim still thought that she was beautiful. "Yeah, I saw her. What about it?" Jim mumbled.

"I'm just saying. She might be your type," answered Scott. Ever since Jim's girlfriend had broken up with him a month before, his friends had been trying to fix him up with somebody new. They wanted him to get a date before prom, so that the whole group could go together.

Jim shrugged, eager to change the subject. He was still upset about the breakup, and he wasn't anxious to get hurt again. As far as he was concerned, the guys could go to the prom without him.

Although Jim tried to keep Maria out of his mind that day, she came into his thoughts anyway, at the unlikeliest times. He thought of her while he was walking to class, and remembered her shy smile as he was spinning the combination of his locker.

Walking home that afternoon, Jim looked up and saw that Maria was just a few yards in front of him. His stomach dropped, and his mouth went dry. Should he try to speak to her? He didn't want to seem weird. After all, they didn't even know each other. Jim was still debating with himself when he realized that he'd begun walking faster and was now almost at Maria's side. She shot him a quick glance and then looked back down at the ground. There was something so sad and lonely in the gesture that Jim decided he would speak to her. After all, it must be terrible to be at a new school and not know anyone.

"Hi," he said. The word caught in his throat and came out sounding like a cough. He tried to start over. "I—I'm Jim," he said.

Maria looked up at him for a moment without answering. Although the sun was hidden behind clouds, she squinted as if the light hurt her eyes. She stared at him and seemed to be trying to decide something. Finally, she spoke.

"My name is Maria," she said in a voice that was barely a whisper. Jim felt something come over him, some kind of tenderness for the girl with the soft, tiny voice.

"Maria," he repeated. He wanted to put his arms around her right then, but of course, he knew he couldn't. He didn't know what else to say, but Maria didn't seem to mind the silence. Nor did she seem to mind when he missed his own turn and kept walking beside her through town, all the way to her driveway.

"This is where I live," she said when they got there. Jim snapped back to reality and realized where they were.

"You live…up there?" he asked. They were standing at the foot of the hill that led up to the old Mason place. It was a crumbling mansion that Jim thought nobody had lived in for years. He didn't know why, but it had always given him a chilly feeling to look at that place.

"Thank you for seeing me home," Maria said. Then she turned and headed up the driveway. As Jim walked home, he felt like he was in some kind of trance. He skipped dinner that night and went straight to bed, where he dreamed of her.

—

The next day, Jim avoided Scott and the rest of the guys. He couldn't think about anything except Maria, and he didn't think that his friends would understand. Maria wasn't like any of the other girls Jim had dated, and he couldn't talk about her in the same way. He felt protective of her, like he didn't want anyone else to know things about her. He thought of the sound of her voice and the way that her hair seemed to swallow up light like a black hole, and he imagined that these things were secrets, for only him to know.

In math class, Jim gave up his regular seat next to his friend Dave and sat in the empty one next to Maria. When Dave came in he gave Jim a questioning look. Jim just shrugged his shoulders and looked away. Although Maria didn't speak to him at all during math class, Jim felt satisfied just being near her. When the bell rang, he grabbed onto her sleeve as she picked up her books. Startled, Maria turned to face him.

"Sorry," Jim said. "I was just wondering, can I walk you home again today?" She didn't answer. "Please?"

"Alright," she said.

"Where should I meet you?" Jim asked. But Maria had already walked away.

—

He found her after the final bell, walking in the direction of her house. She hadn't waited on him.

"Hey," he said, jogging to catch up with her.

"Hello."

"I thought I was going to walk you home."

"Oh, I apologize. I've haven't felt well these past few days, and I suppose that I forgot," Maria said, but Jim didn't think that her words rang true.

"That's okay."

They walked along in silence again. Jim wondered how he could have such strong feelings for Maria when in truth, they had never really even had a whole conversation. As they neared her house, he started to think about all of the things he wanted to say, and about how he wouldn't see Maria again until the next day. He decided to tell her the things that he felt, as best he could.

"Maria," he said, "I know that this is happening so fast, but I can't help it. I haven't been able to stop thinking about you. I don't know why. What is it about you?"

Maria shrugged reluctantly. Jim had the strange feeling that this wasn't the first time she'd heard this kind of talk. He went on. "I'm serious. I don't know what it is, but there's something special about you. Something kind of—I don't know—haunting."

Jim's face burned. The words sounded silly to him even as he said them. He was afraid that Maria would laugh at him, but she didn't. She didn't even seem to think that what he'd said was strange. She looked at his face, and her expression was pained and sad.

"Jim, I'm afraid that I'm fond of you too. I like you very much. I wish that wasn't the case."

"What? Why? Maria, this could be a good thing! I feel the same way about you. What's wrong with that?"

Maria started to cry. "It's not a good thing. Please believe me, Jim, I can only hurt you. It's the only thing that I'm good for. Please, just leave me alone."

Jim felt his heart breaking. "No, Maria. Don't cry. What's the matter?" He stretched out his arms to hold her, but to his dismay, Maria was already gone, headed in the direction of her house. Jim was dumbstruck. He stood in the same spot for a full ten minutes, until the gray sky broke open and started to rain. Only then did he turn and walk slowly back toward home.

—

In math class the next day, Jim was in his seat five minutes before the bell rang. He was hoping that he could talk to Maria before class started, but she never showed up. He looked for her afterward in the hall and at her locker, but she was nowhere to be found.

That afternoon, Jim walked by himself to the old Mason place. At the bottom of the hill, he stopped and took a deep breath, trying to gather his nerve. The house was definitely creepy; he hadn't imagined that. It was at least three stories high, made of stone, and seemed to be falling apart. Jim swallowed hard and then marched up the driveway.

The bell didn't work when he tried to ring it, so Jim knocked on the door. Quietly at first, and then harder when no one answered. He was about to walk away when the door swung open with a tired creak. Maria stood in the doorway looking pale and sad, but somehow more beautiful than Jim had ever seen her.

"Maria. I had to see you. When you didn't show up at school today, I…I…" Jim felt a knot in his throat.

"I'm sick. Quite sick, actually." Jim realized again how different she was from other girls. She didn't even speak the same way. Her words sounded formal and old-fashioned. He stared at her quizzically.

"What's the matter? Should I call a doctor? Where are your parents?" Jim was getting frantic. He tried to stick his head inside the door, but Maria blocked him.

"No! Don't come in here. You must go away right now!"

But Jim insisted. He pushed his way inside the dimly lit house. Maria relented.

Immediately, Jim was struck with the feeling that they had stepped back in time. There was no evidence of modern technology in the house. No television, stereo, or digital clocks. Everything seemed coated in a thin layer of dust.

"Wow. This place is…" Jim didn't know how to continue.

"Strange? I know," Maria filled in for him.

"I wasn't going to say that. It's just different. It looks like something from the movies. Don't your parents have a TV?"

"I don't have either of those things."

"Huh?"

"I don't have a TV. And I don't have parents."

"You're…you're an orphan?"

Maria hesitated. "Not exactly. Tell me, when were you born? What year?"

"1981. But what does that have to do with anything?"

"I will tell you, since you refuse to leave. This will be difficult to understand. But please do try. You see, I was born a very, very long time ago. I used to have parents. They're dead now."

"Oh. I'm sorry to hear that." He wondered what had happened to them, and why she didn't sound more upset about it.

"I've had some time to get over their deaths. I've had many, many years." Jim was too confused to say anything, so he just waited until she went on.

"This will be difficult to believe, Jim, but I was born in the late part of the nineteenth century. In 1898, to be exact. My parents died of the Spanish flu in 1919."

"Okay. So you're like a hundred years old. That's

okay. I like older women." Jim tried to laugh. Maria didn't.

"I assure you, I am not joking, Jim."

"Yeah, okay. Sure, Maria." Jim stood up to leave. He didn't like having his leg pulled.

"It's true. But by the time they died, I was already…changed."

"Changed?"

"Yes. When I was sixteen years old, I fell in love for the first time. He was a young farmhand named Daniel who came to work for my parents in the year 1914. He was beautiful. I began to sneak outside late at night to see him, in the barn. It wasn't long before he told me his secret."

"What secret?" Jim felt sick to his stomach. He wasn't sure that he wanted to know the answer.

"Daniel was a vampire. The living dead. He fed off the blood of living things." Maria took a deep breath. "And in time, so did I."

Jim felt dizzy. He wanted to think that Maria was lying, but deep inside, he knew it was the truth.

"I forbade him to take my parents. I would not let him do to them what I'd allowed him to do to me. For several years, we lived this way in secret, going out at night to feed on my father's livestock." A tear welled up in Maria's eye. But then, when my parents became sick and died, we were so hungry, and I yearned for my first taste of human blood. They were dead, and I knew that we could no longer hurt them, so we drank their blood."

Maria paused for a little while, shaking with sobs. "After that, I was so ashamed and so horrified that I sent

Daniel away. I shut myself up in this house and vowed never to leave again. For more than a hundred years, I've kept that promise. I've lived off animal blood—rats and stray dogs, and never a drop of human blood since that day."

"But," Jim said, "you came out again."

She nodded. "The hunger became too strong. I came looking for another person to feed me."

Jim's voice caught in his throat. "M—me?" he stuttered. Maria nodded.

"At first I considered it. You made yourself so available, coming here again and again. But I cannot do it. You remind me too much of Daniel. I still love him, and because of that, I will not hurt you."

There was a long silence. Maria broke it. "So go, Jim. Please, you must go. Before I cannot help myself." Jim felt torn, thinking about how lovely and special Maria was, and how much he wanted to be with only her. But then he noticed the hungry look in her eye.

This time, Jim did what she said. He jumped from his seat and ran out the door and down the driveway.

BITTERSWEET REVENGE

Diana opened the oven to check on dinner and caught a delicious whiff of roasted vegetables and chicken. Mmmm, almost done. She turned the dial down to warm, then uncorked the red wine and poured two glasses, leaving them on the counter to breathe. She paced around the kitchen for a moment trying to think of what last minute touches she might have forgotten.

With nothing left to do, she walked back into her bedroom to check her appearance in the full length mirror. She couldn't help but be pleased with herself. Her blond hair hung like a silky sheet partway down her back, and her red velvet dress clung seductively to her hips and waist. Diana smiled into the mirror, making sure that she didn't have any lipstick on her teeth. She settled into an armchair to wait on Ryan, who should be there any minute. Everything that night would be perfect. Well, almost perfect…

The doorbell rang, rousing Diana from a deep sleep. She looked at the red lights of her digital alarm clock. Eleven o'clock. Oh, Ryan, she thought, with fresh anger seeping through her sleepy state. She ran her fingers through her hair, flung the door open wide, and glared at her boyfriend, who stood there holding a dozen white roses, a pitiful look softening his usually intense green eyes.

Diana sighed. She took the roses, accepting a kiss on the cheek, but not returning it. She turned around and walked toward the kitchen. The chicken and vegetables, once pulled from the oven, were dry as dust. One of the wine glasses had attracted a fruit fly, which floated facedown in the blood-colored liquid. Diana herself had not held up well either. The nap had left crease marks on her cheek and smudged her mascara.

"Well, Ryan, welcome to our romantic anniversary dinner. You can serve yourself. I'm not hungry anymore." She picked up the glass without the fruit fly in it, walked over and plopped herself down on the couch, folding her arms across her chest.

Ryan stepped quietly up behind her and bent down. "I'm sorry, love," he whispered, the airy words brushing Diana's ear and sending a chill through her. She was determined not to speak. Ryan continued. "I was thinking of you the whole time."

"How can that be true?" Diana asked. "You were with another woman!"

Of course, Ryan didn't deny it. Diana had known for a long time that it was necessary for Ryan to see other women, but that didn't ease the pain. He went on, his smooth words massaging her hurt. With soft fingers, Ryan brushed the hair away from Diana's ear and whispered into it again. "I took her down to the lake. The moonlight on the water made me think of your hair. And above us, there was a magnolia blooming. The white petals were so much like your skin. That's why I stopped for the roses."

Diana closed her eyes to keep the tears from falling. It seemed that she had gotten herself into an impossible situation. The man she loved was not like other men. He was a vampire, kept alive only by drinking human blood. He loved Diana, but he had to seek out other women if he wanted to feed, to live. How could she deny him that?

As he continued to whisper into her ear, Diana felt her resistance fading. As she fell into his deep, soft kiss, Diana relaxed and enjoyed herself. Ryan's kisses were always gentler when he'd just eaten.

—

Ryan promised to make it up to Diana by spending the next day doing whatever she wanted to do. They started off with a nice champagne brunch at Lulu's, followed by a walk in the botanical gardens just outside of town. The weather was beautiful, Ryan was charming, and it was easy for Diana to forget, at least temporarily, how much she'd been bothered by last night's episode.

They caught a matinee and then had an early dinner on a private outdoor terrace at a five-star restaurant. Diana ordered a spinach salad, while Ryan had a filet mignon, cooked rare. As the sun began to set, Diana noticed a familiar shadow falling across Ryan's face. She knew that he would be leaving soon. She took his hand in hers.

"Please, Ryan, not tonight," she pleaded. "Just stay with me, alright?"

He shook his head. "Darling, you know why I can't do that. Trust me, there's nothing in the world I want more than to stay with you, to rest, and sleep in your arms. But I am a creature of the night. There's nothing I can do to change that."

"It isn't fair," she pouted.

"Love never is."

"You've said that before. It doesn't help."

Ryan rose from his chair, and leaned down next to Diana's. Looking up at her with his clear green eyes, he pulled her in for a kiss that warmed her from her ears to her toes. "Does that help?" he asked.

As much as Diana hated to admit it, it did.

—

Later that night, Diana sat on her couch in sweatpants, eating popcorn and watching a bad horror movie on cable. All of a sudden, her anger returned with full force. Look at me, she thought. This is pathetic. My boyfriend is out sucking the necks of other women, and I'm sitting here on my butt eating popcorn. She decided that she was fed up, and this had to stop.

Jumping up from the couch, she brushed a few stray popcorn kernels off herself. She poured a glass of wine, turned on some music, and went to get ready. Half an hour later, Diana looked stunning. She'd chosen a slinky black dress with a low neckline, and she'd piled her blond hair into an appealing knot on top of her head. When she heard her cab pull up in front of the house, she walked out of the door into the dark, warm night, ready for anything.

—

She arrived at Queen's Tavern, a high-class restaurant and bar known for its snooty waiters and custom martinis.

Diana chose a stool near the end of the bar where she could scope out the other patrons, and she ordered a ginger martini, her favorite. The other customers at the bar were mostly men, wealthy, and middle-aged. One of them had a tan line on his finger revealing that he'd removed his wedding ring. None of the men particularly interested Diana. That is, until she saw the man sitting at the opposite end of the bar, staring at her.

He looked nothing like Ryan, though he was equally attractive. He had tousled blond hair and warm brown eyes. He struck Diana as someone who might coach a soccer team and have a golden retriever waiting on him at home. He noticed her staring and smiled. Diana returned the smile shyly. The man picked up his drink and wandered over to her.

"Would you mind if I joined you?" he asked. "I was supposed to meet a friend here, but I seem to have been stood up."

"Of course. Have a seat. I'm sorry about your friend."

"Who knows? It might have been a blessing in disguise," he said with a grin. His smile was warm, and it put Diana at ease. Going out on the town alone wasn't something she did often—actually, she'd never done it, and she was relieved to have found someone so nice and normal to talk to. All the nightly news reports, not to mention her own mother, would have led her to believe that this town was filled with nothing but perverts and predators.

The evening went on nicely. It turned out that Diana's hunches about the man, whose name was David, had been partially right. He was not a soccer coach but a second grade teacher, and instead of a golden retriever, he had a chocolate lab. The conversation flowed so easily that Diana was shocked to look down at her watch and see that it was nearly midnight.

"Oh, my. I didn't realize how late it had gotten. I'd better get going." She paused, then added, "I've had a wonderful time with you, David."

"So have I. Do you really have to go home now? It's Saturday. Surely you don't have to get up too early on Sunday."

"Well, no, but if I wait much longer I might have trouble finding a cab back home."

"Oh come on, live a little. I know this lake just a mile or so from here. The view's amazing at night. We could go take a look at it, then I can give you a lift home."

"Oh, I don't know," Diana hesitated. It was one thing to sit at the bar and have a friendly chat with a stranger, but quite another to get in his car and drive off to the lake. She had gone out that night with the intention of having a little fun, meeting some interesting people, but she never planned on taking it that far.

On the other hand, there was something so welcoming and warm about David's manner. He didn't seem like a dangerous type. The two martinis Diana had drunk by that point gave her an additional illusion of security, and she wasn't using her best judgment. Suddenly the idea of sitting by the lake with David seemed like just the thing she needed.

"Okay. Let's do it." She grabbed her handbag and followed David to his car.

—

As it turned out, David was right about the view. He took her hand and led her over to a bench. As they looked out over the quiet water of the lake, Diana noticed the moonlight on the still water and thought about what Ryan had said the night before. The moonlight on the water made me think of your hair… She was seized by nostalgia and regret. She'd acted horribly. This whole night had been just to make Ryan jealous. Diana realized that now.

"David, I've made a mistake. I need to go home now."

"Why? What's the matter?"

"Never mind. I'm sorry. It's not you. But would you mind taking me home now?"

"Come on, now. Cheer up. We just got here." He gave her a playful tickle in the ribs, which just made her feel even more guilty. She sat there like a stone, not smiling, but David kept on. His body language was playful and aggressive at the same time, and Diana was wondering what she'd gotten herself into, and how she was going to get out of it.

"Okay, okay, I get the point. You don't look like you're having much fun. I'll make you a deal. Let me tell you a secret, a really quick one, and then we'll go."

Diana was annoyed at the strange request, but she shrugged. Anything to get home. "Fine," she said. "What is it?"

He leaned in to her ear and whispered. "I'm a vampire," he said with a high pitched laugh. "And now, you will be too."

Before Diana could react, David had planted his face in

her neck. If she hadn't been so afraid, it might have almost tickled, the way that his lips bit playfully at her skin. When he bared his teeth and pierced her vein, Diana sat as still as a stunned rat, while the man sucked at her neck. She couldn't scream or move or cry. She just waited for it to be over, hoping that she'd make it out alive. She wondered through a haze of fear if this was how Ryan spent his nights, and if this was what the women felt for him.

—

But when she awoke the next morning in her own bed, not knowing how she'd gotten there, the fear was gone. Diana felt renewed, powerful, and above all, she felt hungry. She knew that there was only one thing that would satisfy her, and she had to have it. Oh Ryan, she thought. I understand. How could I ever have not understood?

She lifted the phone's receiver and dialed her boyfriend's familiar number. He answered groggily. Diana understood that he had been out late the night before, feeding, and she was jealous. "Darling," she whispered into the phone. "Please come over. I need you. Come here, and teach me everything you know."

THE ANNIVERSARY GIFT

To the casual observer, Beverly and Raymond Norton seemed like many other couples of their age and social standing. They were elegant, thin, expensive-looking people who appeared to be in their late fifties. They both had dark hair, threaded tastefully for their age with strands of silver. They lived in a mansion on a cliff that overlooked the city lights. They drove expensive cars, donated to charity, and sat on the boards of prominent artistic foundations.

Their marriage, like many high-society marriages, seemed to be based on compatibility and wealth, rather than any great passion. The Nortons didn't fight or kiss in public. Their friends, family, and acquaintances just naturally assumed that they were content with each other, if a little bored. All of these were illusions that the Nortons had worked for years to create. They knew what people thought of them, and they wanted to keep it that way.

For the truth was, Beverly and Raymond Norton had a secret. A dark secret that stretched back hundreds of years, and was shrouded in murder and blood. The Nortons, like so many of those seemingly normal citizens who walk among us, were vampires.

Even their closest friends did not know this about them. Of course, people wondered why they never seemed to age, but this was usually chalked up to healthy living and the wonders of plastic surgery. Whenever the Nortons were in a place long enough for people to truly become suspicious, they would tell their friends that they were taking an extended cruise, pack up a few belongings, and leave a place, never to return again. Money was not a problem. The Nortons had been members of a royal family back in the old country, and they still had stores of gold stashed in various places, in sums that would be nearly unimaginable in these days. They had no children, which worked out well for them. There was no one around to force them into answering uncomfortable questions.

Though all of these things might be surprising facts to people who thought they knew the Nortons, perhaps the best kept secret of all was that the Nortons were deeply, truly, and passionately in love with each other.

—

That weekend would be the Norton's wedding anniversary, and Raymond wanted to get something very special for Beverly. He went to a jeweler downtown and began looking around for the perfect gift for his wife.

That's when he noticed Missy Weaver. In fact, the sales clerk already knew who Raymond Norton was. He came into the store fairly often, at least every few months. Missy always made it a point to take note of which regular customers paid with platinum credit cards. Those were the ones whose names she learned, and Raymond Norton was one of them.

"Mr. Norton," she cooed. "May I help you with something?"

Raymond looked her over. She was a beautiful young woman, right at the age where loveliness peaked. Her tan skin stretched smoothly over her high, strong cheekbones. Her flushed lips parted appealingly to reveal a tiny edge of tongue and a few of her straight, white teeth. Missy wasn't unaware of this; it was a little pose she'd mastered by practicing in the mirror for hours.

"I'm looking for a gift for my wife," he said, his gaze scanning Missy's curvy shape and coming to rest on her wide blue eyes.

"Oh, how nice. Is there a special occasion?"

"Yes, it's our anniversary."

"Wonderful! How long have you been married?"

Mr. Norton let out a chuckle under his breath. "You wouldn't believe me if I told you, young lady."

"Well, maybe you'll be interested in one of these." Missy unlocked a glass case and pulled out a tray of the store's most extravagant pieces. Gaudy diamond broaches, heavy rings, hair clips that sparkled blindingly in the overhead light. While he was looking the pieces over, he asked Missy how she'd known his name. The young girl began to blush. Calling customers by their names was a tactic that could be either flattering or awkward.

"Oh, I don't. I mean—I just—" Missy kept stammering. Raymond looked up, amused by her embarrassment, and quite taken by the pink flush that had crept into her cheeks.

Raymond selected a ring, a huge ruby flanked by smaller diamonds. "I'll take this one." As he placed it in

Missy's hand, he let his touch linger there longer than it needed to. Missy, smiling, did not seem to mind.

As Raymond left the store, he took a card from his wallet and handed to the girl. "My wife is on a cruise for the weekend—it was an anniversary gift from me. Perhaps, if you're free Saturday night, you might stop by. My phone number is on the card. Call me if you'd like directions." Then, with a smile, he walked out of the store.

Missy could hardly believe her luck. At most, she'd hoped for a little back-and-forth flirting between herself and Mr. Norton. If he thought she was cute, he'd ask for her when he came in, and that would boost her commissions. The fact that he'd actually asked her out was unbelievable. It wasn't that she was particularly attracted to the older man, but going to his home definitely sounded like a good idea. Missy had a few friends who'd dated older, rich men, some of them married, and she knew that was the type of man that gave the best presents, by far. Maybe Mr. Norton—Raymond, rather—would even have something nice for her Saturday night.

—

Missy was right on time Saturday night. Raymond opened the door himself, and found her standing there with a shy look on her face. She was wearing a low cut dress and too much makeup. Her attempts to look grown up made Raymond painfully aware of just how young she actually was. He chastised himself inwardly for what he was going to do, but he knew it was inevitable. After all, everyone had needs.

"My dear, come in," he said, putting an arm around her

shoulder and shepherding her into the hallway. "May I fix you a drink? Some wine, perhaps?"

"Wine would be great," Missy squeaked. She'd felt so mature as she rode in her cab up to the mansion. She was all dressed up, perhaps on her way to her first affair with a married man. But once she stepped inside that palatial home with its marble and chandeliers, she felt like a naïve, bumbling child. Part of her just wanted to turn and run back in the direction she'd come from. But the other part looked at the splendor around her, and wondered if some small part of it could ever be hers. She decided to stay.

Raymond led her into an expansive living room and gestured toward a couch. She sat down, the huge leather cushions nearly swallowing her up. Raymond poured a glass of wine, his back toward her at the bar. Soft music was being piped in from somewhere, although Missy couldn't determine its source. Now that's class, she thought, as Raymond settled in on the couch next to her. "I just love your place," she gushed. "Have you lived here long?"

"Oh yes, quite awhile. But we like it."

There was a long silence between them. Missy had no idea what to say to this man. They didn't have much in common, after all. So she looked down and concentrated on sipping her wine, which was very good.

"Missy, dear, I want to thank you for helping me find the perfect present for my wife. I know that she's going to be so pleased."

Missy nodded. She wasn't used to drinking wine, and it had started to make her feel dizzy. "You're welcome. I hope your wife likes the ring."

"No, not the ring." Missy was sinking deeper into the couch, and as Raymond looked down at her, his expression was eager. She wondered what he meant about the ring. Was she confused about what he'd bought? She could have sworn it was the ring with the rubies. "I've selected a different gift for my wife," Raymond said.

At that moment, Beverly Norton's footsteps padded down the hall and into the living room. "Did I hear someone talking about me?" she asked in a silky, luxuriant voice.

"What—what's going on?" Missy asked. Her words felt fuzzy and far away as she said them.

Beverly ignored her question. "Oh, Raymond, you didn't! My gift! She's absolutely breathtaking." The older woman crouched over Missy and ran a long red fingernail across the girl's smooth cheek. Missy's eyes were getting almost too heavy to hold open.

Raymond looked at Beverly, his beautiful wife. He was always amazed that after so many years, she could still make his heart beat faster. "I hope that you enjoy your gift. She should be feeling very sleepy by now." Raymond put his arms around his wife and kissed her deeply. "Happy anniversary, darling."

"Yes. Happy anniversary."

THE KISS

"Isn't he just adorable?" whispered Candy.

"So sweet," agreed Gina. The two girls were high school volunteers at Shady Grove Nursing Home, and they were talking about Henry, another volunteer. The reason they thought Henry was so cute is that he was ninety-two years old.

"I mean, I hope that when I'm that age, I can still be as active as Henry."

"I know. And he's so cheerful! He actually seems to want to be here."

"Which is more than I can say for the two of us. Right, Gina?"

Gina rolled her eyes in agreement. The two girls were volunteering only because of a community service requirement in their high school's honor society.

They were right about Henry, though. He did love his job. Every afternoon, he put on his scrubs and walked over to the home, which was only two blocks away from his apartment. There, he made his rounds bringing the residents their meals and seeing if they needed anything extra, like someone to sit and talk for a while, or play a hand of cards with them. Even though Henry was a

57

volunteer and not making any money for his work, he felt immensely rewarded by it. It gave him the will to get out of bed every morning. He wouldn't have traded his job for anything in the world.

One of the extra benefits of working at Shady Grove was that Henry got to see Greta every day. Greta was eighty-nine, and if you asked Henry, still a beauty. Of course, she was wrinkled now, much smaller and frailer than she used to be, but she also had an inner glow that radiated out of her. It was uncommon to see that glow in people Greta's age. Normally it had been lost long before then.

Henry knocked softly on Greta's door, holding an aluminum tray of food. "Hello, dear," he said, cracking the door.

"Come in, Henry," Greta called. Before he even saw her face, he could tell by her voice that she was smiling. That was another thing that he loved about Greta.

"You're looking simply radiant today," Henry commented as he set the food tray down on the table across Greta's bed.

"Why thank you! What do we have here today?" she asked, surveying the food. "Oh, my favorites! Barbecued ribs, corn on the cob, and some peanut brittle for dessert. Why Henry, you're an angel." Henry chuckled at her joke. Actually, the tray held some creamed ham, grayish mashed potatoes, and a plastic cup of cubed peaches.

"Only the best for you, Greta dear."

"Henry, I can't tell you how your visits cheer me up. It can get lonely sitting in this bed all day. You're so lucky that you still have your health. What I wouldn't give to be able to walk around and visit all afternoon, like you do!"

"Well, then make a wish, Greta. You never know. It just might come true."

—

"Henry, it's almost eight. Are you going home soon?" asked Candy. She and Gina were packing up their things to leave, having dutifully put in their three hours of work.

"No, you young ladies go on ahead. I promised Mr. Sheehan that I'd play some rummy with him. I can let myself out."

"Okay, see you tomorrow, then." Giggling to themselves again about how cute Henry was, the girls headed for the door.

Henry waited awhile at the information desk, checking to see if there would be any visitors arriving that evening. It would be rare for anyone other than the full-time staff to be at the nursing home that late, but it was better to be safe than sorry.

Next, he wandered around the hallways, taking stock of where all the staff were at the moment. Nora was on call at the main nurse's station, reading a magazine. Mr. Nelson was sweeping the far wing of the home, and the remaining two nurses were having coffee in the break room. "Hi Henry," they called to him as he walked by. He waved back, and continued down the hall to Felicity Donner's room.

Henry opened the door quietly and stepped inside. The room was dark and it smelled like sweat and mildew. On the television, there was a live feed of a congressional session, but Felicity Donner was not watching it. Her head was turned to the side wall, and her eyes were fixed on the window in a dull stare. Henry couldn't tell if she'd heard him come in or not. He sat down in a chair by the bed and took her hand in his. Her eyes flickered.

"Mrs. Donner, can you hear me?" Henry whispered. The old woman nodded weakly and tried to say something.

"What was that?" Henry leaned in closer to hear her small voice.

"I said, is it time?"

"Yes, love. It's time."

"Oh. Good." Mrs. Donner closed her eyes. A tiny smile broke on her lips.

For months, she had been asking for Henry's help. Mrs. Donner was in a lot of pain. She had long ago lost that light in her eyes. The time for her death was coming, but it was coming too slowly and painfully for her to bear. One day, Henry had revealed that yes, he could help her, and that in allowing him to do so, she would also be helping him.

"Bless you, Mrs. Donner," Henry said. "Soon you will be at peace."

Henry squeezed the old woman's hand and pushed up her loose sleeve. It was important that the wounds not be seen, and so he had to avoid the neck. He leaned forward and wrapped his mouth around Mrs. Donner's frail arm. His jaws, teeth, and lips were astonishingly strong for a man of his age. With one firm bite, he began to draw out what life remained in Felicity Donner. For the first time in many years, Felicity felt something, too. A deep thrill running the entire length of her. It might have been pleasure or pain; Felicity felt numb for so long that she couldn't feel the difference, and it didn't matter to her. When he finished, Henry pulled down her sleeve, wiped his mouth, and kissed Mrs. Donner on the forehead before leaving the room.

When the nursing attendants found her dead the next day, the look on the old woman's face was rapturous.

—

"It's very sad about Mrs. Donner," Greta said to Henry the next day. He was sitting by her bed, holding a ball of thread still for her as she crocheted.

"Do you really think so, Greta?" he asked. Death was so common in the nursing home that few people ever seemed truly saddened by it. And given the state that some of the patients were in, death was sometimes even viewed as a blessing.

"Yes. I think it's sad when anyone dies. There's just so much to live for in this world."

"But for some people, it isn't so. Maybe Mrs. Donner didn't think so. Maybe she was ready to go."

"Yes, that's true. She seemed ready, and in that way, I'm glad for her. But if I had my way, I'd go on living forever." Greta laughed as she added, "Maybe then I'd be able to finish this doily someday!"

"Greta, what if you could live forever? Would you really want that?"

"Oh, yes. I think that I would!"

"Well, maybe it could be done."

"What do you mean, Henry? You're not going senile on me, are you?" She laughed.

"No, I assure you, I'm not. What if I told you I would give you a kiss to make you live forever?"

"Why, Henry. I'd think you were trying to steal a kiss from a helpless old lady." When he didn't answer, she added, "It'd have to be one heck of a kiss."

"It would be." With that, he drew his face in close to Greta's. "It might sting a little, though."

Greta's voice was wispy when she answered. "That's alright."

Henry put his mouth to hers and kissed, taking one of her lips between his strong, sharp teeth. The blood that he drew from her lip was the sweetest he'd ever tasted. "Oh, my Greta," he whispered.

"Henry." She kissed him back, engaging in a bite of her own. Their blood commingled, and Greta felt more alive than she'd felt in a very long time. When the kiss was over, she lay back in her bed and smiled.

"Is it true, then? Will I live forever now?"

"Yes, you will. Do you regret it?"

Greta considered. She felt blood coursing through her veins, and the strength she'd lost sitting in that nursing home bed for years seemed to have returned to her. "No," she said honestly. "I don't regret it at all."

—

Late that night, Henry used his key to sneak back into the nursing home. He told Nora, still sitting at the nurse's station, that he'd forgotten something in his locker in the back. I hope I have that kind of energy when I'm his age, thought Nora. Out of bed at eleven o'clock at night. She went back to reading her magazine, and didn't even notice that Henry didn't come back through. She was so caught up in a magazine about giving middle-aged skin back its youthful glow, that she didn't hear the side door open as Henry and Greta stole out of it, into the night.

DIGGING

It was a cold, clear night, just the kind of night that Sam liked for working. Most people didn't know it, but the graveyard could be the most peaceful place in the world on a night like that. To Sam, there was nothing menacing or scary about it—the quiet air, the green expanses, and all the people sleeping beneath the quiet earth. Sam would never trade his job for one where he had to deal with rude customers or busybody managers. One thing about dead people, he often thought, is that they never complain.

And tonight, that was a very good thing. Sam had some business to take care of, and it was just as well that nobody see what he needed to do. His wife, Eliza, had been pestering him just that day about a broach she wanted.

"A broach?" Sam had asked. "You're a gravedigger's wife. What in the devil's name would you do with a broach, woman?"

"What? I can't have nice things because I'm married to you? I could have been a banker's wife, but I chose you instead. Don't you owe me something for that?"

Sam had wanted to ask exactly which banker she'd ever had a shot with, but he bit his tongue, saying instead,

"It's hard enough getting by on the money I make. We can barely afford to fix the car, and you want to go off spending money on jewelry you'll have no place to wear."

Eliza had moaned and groaned at him for so long that eventually he gave in. "Alright!" he'd said. "If it's a broach you want, it's a broach you'll get." He hadn't mentioned anything about which broach she'd get, but he had one in mind.

Grave digging had gotten a lot easier since they got the backhoes. Sam had been doing it for so long that he remembered the days when it was just the men and their shovels. It took three or four of them working all night to dig a grave back in those days, but since the backhoe, he could do it himself in just minutes. Not to mention it was a lot easier on his own back, which was a blessing. Through a lifetime of hard work, Sam's body had taken about all the abuse it could handle.

That night, he was set to work the Vanderkamp grave. It was a fresh one, dug just a week before for a woman about thirty years old. Sam had worked the funeral himself, and as he positioned the coffin to be lowered in the ground, he thought to himself what a pity it was that such a beautiful young woman should meet her end so soon. There was no mention at the funeral of how she died, and Sam had been unable to imagine what could have happened. She didn't look ill, and there was no sign of physical violence to her body. In fact, Sam remembered thinking that she looked almost alive, without the waxy shine of death on her. She was unlike anyone that Sam had ever seen.

He hated that he was about to dig up her grave and disturb her peaceful slumber. But on the other hand, if he didn't get Eliza what she wanted soon, he'd never hear the end of it.

As Sam put the backhoe into gear, he thought of the broach that the young woman had been buried in. It was an intricate bed of seed pearls set in gold, probably an antique, and nothing like the ruby and emerald piece that Eliza had her eyes on. But if she complained, Sam would just tell her that beggars can't be choosers, and she was lucky to get anything at all. Maybe, for once, she would not argue back with him.

After a while, Sam heard the distinctive sound of the bucket scraping on wood, and he knew he'd hit the coffin. He'd dug the whole wide enough so that he could lift the lid off it himself, without having to raise it off the ground, and so he climbed down into the hole and started to do so. He readied himself and took a deep breath, then held it. He knew what a body could smell like when it had been dead this long, and it was not a smell he wanted to inhale deeply.

What he found when he lifted the lid took his breath away.

There was the woman, looking just as she had when Sam put her in the ground a week ago. Her red hair was still smooth and bright, and her skin was as fresh as a child's. Sam took a tentative breath and found that even the smell coming from the coffin was pleasant, a clean green kind of scent. He had expected to find Ms. Vanderkamp in a rather disgusting state of decay, but instead, here she was, looking just like a sleeping young girl.

"Well, if that isn't the strangest thing," Sam said, shaking his head.

Mesmerized by the beautiful woman, Sam almost forgot the reason why he'd opened the coffin. But then he saw the broach pinned to her chest. The tiny pearls glowed like the moonlight cast upon them. Shaking himself out of the spell, Sam hurriedly unpinned the broach and put it in his pocket. As he did, the woman inside opened her eyes.

Sam had never had such a shock in his life. "I must be dreaming," he mumbled under his breath. Still, he could not get out of that cemetery fast enough. He slammed down the coffin lid without looking at it again, scuttled into the backhoe, and covered the grave.

Sam did not get a wink of sleep that night. Every time he closed his eyes, he saw the redheaded Ms. Vanderkamp, with hers wide open. He stayed in bed until around noon, which is when he normally rose. Feeling that he could avoid his wife no longer, he dutifully got out of bed and went downstairs, where he found Eliza.

"About time you got out of bed," she whined.

"Leave me alone, Eliza. I didn't get a bit of sleep."

"That's your own fault. Playing out in that graveyard, no doubt. I shudder to think about what it is you do out there all night."

"I dig graves, woman. It's my job, and you know it good and well."

Eliza chewed her lip for a moment, seeming to consider something, and then she abruptly changed her tone. "Did you…bring me anything special?" She tried to smile. On her, it looked like a hound dog sucking a lemon.

Sam hesitated. He knew that he had a choice. If he gave Eliza the broach now, she would be off his back for at least a while. She might even allow him to go back to sleep for a while before he had to get back to work that night. On the other hand, he wasn't sure he even wanted to give it to her anymore. After the disturbing events of last night, he didn't like having the broach anywhere near him. He put his hand in his pocket and closed his fingers around it. It seemed to give off a hellish heat. His mind was made up at that moment.

"No. I don't have nothing for you."

He would take the broach back that night and return it to its rightful place.

Sam waited around the house until the deep night had fallen. There were no funerals scheduled for the next day, and so it wouldn't do for him to be seen going into the graveyard and using the equipment. If anyone caught him, he might lose his job. Still, Sam felt that he had to get rid of that broach, and he felt also that it had to go back into the grave it had come from. If not, he had the sense that it might keep haunting him for a long time to come.

And as much as he hated to admit it, Sam was also motivated by what he thought he'd seen in the grave. He needed to go back there and see that the beautiful woman was definitely dead. Otherwise, he might have to live the rest of his life thinking that he might be crazy.

He went through the same motions that he had the night before. Only this time when he held his breath opening the coffin, it was out of anticipation. Sam halfway hoped that he would see a horrible sight—the dead woman, partially decomposed and completely lifeless. But in a deeper, more secret part of himself, he hoped to see what he had seen the night before—that incredibly gorgeous face, with her eyes open.

The woman was just as he remembered her. Skin soft, hair gleaming in the moonlight. The only differences were that her eyes were closed, and the broach, of course, was missing.

Sam wanted to pin the broach to her dress and be done with the whole business, but he found himself prolonging it, wanting to stare for just a few more moments at this lovely creature glowing in the moonlight. Finally, he forced himself to put the broach back on her. As he did, her eyes opened.

"Help me," she whispered in a voice as soft as flower petals. Sam was surprised that he wasn't more frightened. Rather, he felt intrigued by the voice. He wanted the woman—or ghost, or whatever she was—to keep talking.

"Help you what?"

"Help me live."

"Who are you? Are you a ghost?"

"No. I'm a person, like you. They buried me. They buried me because they thought that I was evil." Her eyes were still open, but she hadn't moved otherwise. She looked weak.

"Who buried you?"

"My family."

"Why did you let them do it?"

"I was sick. I still am. I wasn't strong enough to stop them. But you can help me. You can give me strength."

"How can I do that?"

"Kiss me."

Sam was so shocked that he nearly shut the coffin lid on her. Kiss her? No woman had asked Sam to kiss her in more than three decades. He was flattered, excited, and just plain terrified. He still thought that he might be going crazy, too. He'd heard of this kind of thing in children's stories, giving a kiss to a sleeping princess so that she could come back to life. Maybe that's the kind of thing that she wanted.

Sam tried to tell himself that he was doing a good deed, but in truth, he was mostly thinking of the woman's soft lips and pale cheeks. He bent in to kiss her.

"Closer," she whispered. Sam leaned in closer.

His face was almost on top of hers. He puckered his lips to give her the kind of sweet peck that he and Eliza often traded when she was in a better mood. But just as he got close enough, he felt a sharp pain stabbing at his neck.

Sam didn't know what was happening. As Ms. Vanderkamp bled him, she began to get stronger, lifting her hands, holding his body to hers in a grip so tight that he couldn't get away. Sam felt his life draining away. In a way, this didn't surprise him much. The whole experience had been too mysterious, too strange, to have a happy ending.

He was surprised, however, by one thing. As Sam let go of his life, his last thoughts were not of the beautiful redhead sucking at his neck. Instead, they were of his wife,

Eliza. He was filled with one last wave of sadness at the fact that he would never again hear her voice squawking at him, and never get to see her with a beautiful broach pinned to her chest.

JUDGMENT NIGHT

Marcus Riles sat on his bed with his eyes closed as his roommate Todd got ready to go out. It was a small dorm room, and as he smelled the noxious odor of Todd's hair gel, Marcus wished for the thousandth time that his parents had had enough money to get him a private room.

Todd's friend Billy entered the room without knocking. Great, thought Marcus. Billy was a jerk. He hung out in the room often, and for some reason, he was never content to just leave Marcus alone. He always had to bother him or make fun of him. Tonight was no exception.

"Hey goth boy," he said in his cocky, taunting voice. "You coming to the Delta party with us tonight?" He laughed.

"No, Billy," Marcus said dully. "I'm not going to the party."

"Too bad," Billy continued sarcastically. "The ladies will be disappointed, I'm sure." He laughed again.

A few more shirt and belt changes later, Todd was ready to go.

"Later, dude," he said as he walked out. "Have fun with your Internet."

Marcus kept his eyes closed for a long time after they

left, as if he were afraid they might still be there if he opened them. When he was sure they were really gone, he got up and walked over to his computer.

Finally, he said to himself as he turned on the monitor. He didn't like to go online when Todd was around. Todd would ask annoying questions about what he was doing, and why he preferred his "computer" friends to people in the real world.

Marcus never corrected him about how people online were just as "real" as any others, and probably a lot more sincere than Todd's fraternity friends, who most likely wouldn't even hang out with the guy anymore if he stopped paying dues.

Marcus entered his favorite chat room and saw that NightChild was there. He'd been talking to her for a few weeks, and they seemed to have a lot in common. Like Marcus, NightChild went to a small, conservative college, lived with a roommate she didn't like, and identified more with the characters in the vampire stories she read than with the people around her. Nearly every night, they spent hours chatting online. Once, Marcus had even fallen asleep in his computer chair and missed class the next day.

Even though he'd never met her in person, Marcus thought that he might be falling for her.

"Hi," he wrote.

"Hi yourself," she replied.

They chatted for a while, and eventually the conversation got pretty heavy. Marcus took a deep breath, and typed, "I really need to see you." Even as he wrote it, he wondered if he was making a mistake. Things seemed to be going so well between them, and he didn't want to mess it all up. What if she wasn't attracted to him? What if he got nervous and couldn't speak? It was one thing to chat online, when he could take time with what he was writing, and simply hit the delete button if something sounded stupid. Talking in person was harder. There was no way to unsay something after the fact.

"I've been thinking the same thing," wrote NightChild. "But I'm nervous."

Relieved that he wasn't the only one, Marcus wrote, "Why should you be nervous?"

"I just worry that I won't live up to your expectations. What if you don't like what I look like? I've been judged all my life, and I couldn't stand it if you judged me, too."

"No way. I've been judged, too. I know what it feels like. I would never do that to you."

"That's easy to say," she replied.

"Try me. Why don't we just do it?"

The two lived only a few hours apart. NightChild said that her car was pretty new, and so she wouldn't mind driving. They made a plan that she would come down the following weekend, and they would meet in a coffee shop that Marcus knew of. Well, that's that, he thought. He swallowed hard, trying to calm the nervous feeling in his stomach. He would just have to go through with it.

—

The week passed quickly. Marcus could think of nothing but NightChild. That was still how he thought of her, even though he'd finally found out that her name was Justine. She had been embarrassed to tell him that, but they both knew that it would be strange if when they met he still called her by her screen name.

He imagined their first meeting over and over in his mind, with few variations. He would be sitting in the café, drinking black coffee, and probably reading. Then the door would open, and she would walk in. He pictured that she would be tall and thin, with pale skin and rich black hair. In his mind, she looked just like the heroines from the vampire books that they both loved so much. She would be wearing a flowing black dress, and lipstick the color of blood. Their eyes would lock, and both of them would be unaware that the people in the café were staring at them, wondering who this beautiful, exotic girl might be. Everyone would think that they were strange, these two people dressed all in black, so obviously enamored with each other. But Marcus and Nightchild would be so wrapped up that they wouldn't care; they would not even be aware of all these strangers there, judging them.

—

Finally the day of the meeting came. Marcus gave himself a close shave, pulled his long black hair back into a shiny ponytail, and put on his black jeans and black trench coat. He got to the café about ten minutes early so that he could be there waiting when she arrived. His nerves were so high that he ordered a decaf coffee, afraid that caffeine might make his hands even shakier than they already were. He took the coffee to a table in the back corner and waited.

There weren't a lot of people in the café—a few college students sitting together studying, one middle-aged couple drinking tea and reading magazines, seemingly oblivious to each other, and a sorority-type girl with blond hair, a short denim skirt, and a pink blouse. Marcus tried to focus on his magazine, but he couldn't help looking up every few seconds toward the door, in case NightChild came in. After a while, he noticed that the sorority girl seemed to be watching him. He kept looking away, but each time he glanced her way, she was still staring at him.

It was ten minutes after three. Marcus was already angry that NightChild was late, and so this vapid-looking girl's stare annoyed him even more than it normally would have. Heaving a sigh, Marcus got up and walked over to her table.

"Do you have a problem?"

"What do you mean?" she asked. She sounded afraid. Marcus was used to girls like that being afraid of him.

"You're staring at me. Do you have a problem with me?"

"No, of course not. It's just that…"

"It's just that what? You think I'm a freak, and so you have the right to stare at me?"

"No. I was just waiting for someone. I thought that you might be him."

"Oh. Well, obviously, I'm not," he said huffily. As he walked back to his table, she called after him in a voice that was barely a whisper.

"Marcus?"

Slowly, unbelievingly, he turned around. "Justine?"

She nodded, tears beginning to well up in her eyes. Marcus couldn't believe he could have been so mistaken. This girl was nothing like the NightChild he'd pictured.

She had neat blond hair, understated gold jewelry, and shiny, pink lip gloss. She looked just like all the girls that made fun of him at college. He hated girls like her. How could she possibly be the same person that he thought he'd gotten to know so well online?

He walked back to her table, his head bowed. "I'm sorry," he mumbled. It's just that you don't exactly look…" He fumbled to find the right words.

"I don't look like your type?" she filled in. Her words were thick with hurt and anger. "I told you this was a mistake. I knew it. You said that you wouldn't judge me, and that's exactly what you did." With that, she got up and stormed out of the café, not even looking back at him.

—

For days afterward, Marcus felt terrible and confused about the whole thing. He hadn't meant to hurt the girl's feelings, but at the same time, he was angry at her for misrepresenting herself. How could a girl like that call herself NightChild? How could she possibly be into the same things that he was, and still dress like all of the other college girls that he knew?

Night after night, he tried to reach her online, but she ignored his messages. Fine, Marcus thought to himself. That lets me off the hook, anyway. As much as he hated to admit it about himself, he didn't think that he could be involved with someone who looked like her. Sure, she was pretty enough. But her style was so far from what he was attracted to that he didn't even want to give her a second chance. He was only writing to her out of guilt, to say that he was sorry for hurting her feelings.

Finally, one night, she wrote him back.

"You there?"

"Yes." There was a long pause where neither wrote anything. Marcus wasn't sure that there was anything left to say. Then, he thought of how she'd looked with tears in her eyes, and he felt the guilt returning. "I'm sorry if I hurt your feelings," he wrote.

"Whatever. I knew you would. You're just like all the rest," she wrote.

"ME? I'm just like all the rest? What about you? Have you taken a look at yourself? You're the one who looks like everybody else. There are a hundred girls who look just like you at my school."

"Looks can be deceiving," she wrote. "Take you, for example. You try to look all scary and goth, but in reality, you're just a scared little boy, like all the rest. You don't know the first thing about what it means to live a dark life."

"And I suppose you do?" he asked.

"Yes. I do."

Marcus didn't know quite what she meant, but he was intrigued. Justine had pointed right at the secret fear in his heart—that deep down, he was just like all the rest of them, not nearly as rare or misunderstood as he made himself out to be.

"What do you mean by a 'dark life'?"

"Well, I guess you'll never know, now will you?" With that, she signed off, leaving Marcus sitting in front of the computer with his mouth hanging open.

—

It took him three days to get her to talk to him again, but his persistence paid off. Justine finally started speaking to him again, and she reluctantly agreed to see him again in person so that they could talk. This time, though, it was she who called the shots. Marcus would have to drive his battered old car up to her town, and he would have to meet her in a place that she chose.

Justine had insisted on meeting him at night, and so Marcus drove the three hours in the dark, following the directions she'd given him. She wouldn't tell him what kind of place it was, and so Marcus was a little surprised when he pulled up to the final stop, in the parking lot of a deserted elementary school.

Justine was waiting for him in the parking lot, the moon shining on her blond hair. "Follow me," she said when he got out of his car. She led him onto the school's playground, an unlit place with rusted swing sets and merry-go-rounds, and a beat-up row of upturned empty tires forming a chain in the pebbly ground.

Despite himself, Marcus felt creeped out. Maybe this girl was stranger than she looked, after all.

She led him over to the merry-go-round, and they sat down next to each other. Although she was still blond, and still dressed in the same preppy style, she looked different to him this time. There was a gleam in her eye that seemed almost malicious, and her sharp teeth, which Marcus hadn't noticed at the café, glinted in the moonlight.

"Is this more what you had in mind?" she whispered. "Is this…dark enough for you?" She smiled in a sinister way that gave Marcus a chill. Suddenly, he was afraid.

"Look, I just wanted to come here to apologize. I shouldn't have judged you the way I did, and I'm sorry."

"Talk, talk, talk," Justine said. "That's not why you came here at all. You came because you thought there was no way someone who looked like me could possibly have a dark secret. You wanted to come and see me, so that you could go on believing that I was the boring one, and you were somehow interesting."

"No, that's not it at all. I just—"

But Justine cut him off with a kiss. Marcus shivered. Her lips were cold as death. She held close to his mouth for a while, and then her lips traveled downward, toward his neck, to the place where his life pulsed within him. She bit, hard.

"You see, Marcus," she said when she withdrew, swiping her hand across her bloody mouth, "I do have a secret. A dark one. And now, you do too. Congratulations. Now you're just like me. As strange as you've always pretended to be. I guess no one ever told you. You should be careful what you wish for."

Marcus was dazed. He didn't know what to do. And so when Justine snuggled up to him, and put her head on his chest, he put his arms around her, and held her tight.

THE FAMILY BUSINESS

Jana didn't even like pizza, but that didn't stop her from eating at Leonardo's at least twice a week.

Of course, it didn't hurt that the most gorgeous man she'd ever seen worked there. His name was Anton, she'd learned from his nametag. He had wolfish blue eyes, dark skin, and naturally curly hair that he held back in a loose ponytail. Jana had never been attracted to a man with a ponytail before. She'd grown up sharing the opinion of her three older brothers—that long hair was strictly for women. So she'd been surprised when, after her first dining experience at Leonardo's, she'd found her thoughts wandering again and again to that long-haired waiter.

Jana couldn't say for sure whether he knew who she was. Leonardo's was a tiny restaurant—usually only two servers on the floor at a time—and Jana always asked for the same table. So far she'd been lucky. Anton had waited on her every time she visited. There was something in his eye and his smile that told her he at least knew her face.

The question was answered one night when Anton approached her table and said in a husky voice that sounded vaguely European, "Back again?"

Jana blushed. "I—I like the pizza," she lied.

Anton was still smiling. He'd probably noticed that she usually just picked at the pizza, then asked for a leftover box. "It must be the sauce."

"Oh, really? Is there something special about the sauce?"

"Yes. There is no garlic."

"No garlic? Why?"

"This is a family-run business, and all of us are allergic to garlic."

"Oh. Well, the sauce is good. I guess I must not like garlic either."

"Of course," he said. She realized that he didn't believe her.

That night, Jana left the restaurant mortified. She made a point of eating three pieces of the pizza. It was rather bland, she realized, now that she knew there was no garlic in it. But she'd rather die than have Anton know she'd only been going there to see him. As she walked the few blocks back to her apartment, she swore to herself that she'd never go back to Leonardo's.

That night, though, she dreamed of Anton. The fact that he'd spoken to her about things that didn't directly concern her dinner had only strengthened her infatuation. She woke up knowing only one thing: she had to see him again. Her pride didn't matter. She would go back there and see him again.

———

The time came even sooner than she'd expected. She planned on waiting a few days, but when she got into her car during her lunch break, she found herself driving toward Leonardo's, almost without any control over what she was doing. She'd never been there during the day and was surprised to find the place closed. There were no lights on, but Jana got out of her car anyway and walked up to the door. It was locked. Strange, she thought. Didn't most restaurants at least have someone there during the afternoon prepping the food or working on the books? Jana got a strange feeling as she backed away from the restaurant and got back into her car. It wasn't just that the restaurant was closed; it looked abandoned, like a place that had been closed down for years. Jana drove back to work, forgetting that she hadn't eaten anything for lunch.

That night, the urge to return to Leonardo's was even stronger than before. She wanted to see Anton of course, but almost as much as that, she wanted to quell her curiosity about the strange place. She walked in and sat at her usual table, and as usual, Anton approached her with a glass of water.

"Hello," he said. His expression was sexy and mysterious, just as it had been the night before. Jana's uneasiness melted away in his faint smile.

"Hi. I tried to come for lunch, but you were closed."

"Oh, yes, we are never open for lunch."

"Why not?"

"It takes a lot of energy to operate a restaurant at night. During the daytime, we sleep."

This sounded to Jana like an odd answer. "What, all of you? All day?"

Anton nodded. "Yes."

There was no further conversation between them until

the meal ended. Jana had forced down two slices of the bland, dry pizza. When Anton approached her with the bill, he spoke again.

"You are a very curious person. You are curious about my family, about our business."

Jana nodded. She couldn't really tell whether he was being flirtatious or confrontational.

"Why don't you stay and find out?"

"What do you mean?"

"After hours. You can stay for a while, as my guest."

Jana didn't trust her voice not to shake. This invitation was more than she could have hoped for. She just nodded her head.

"Good," Anton said. "I will get you something to drink while you wait." He went to the kitchen and came back a few minutes later with a glass of red wine. Anton watched her while she lifted it to her lips and drank. He was still watching her with that characteristic grin.

Jana had trouble not spitting out the wine. It tasted horrible to her. It was thick and tangy, like no wine she'd ever had before.

"The wine is…interesting. What's it made out of?"

"Do you like it? It's the family's private stock. Our favorite wine."

Jana didn't want to be rude, so she had a few more sips as the night went on. As she watched the last customers leaving and the two wait staff cleaning up, she started to feel tipsy. Around midnight, the door opened and in came a very old man and a very old woman. The woman was swathed in a black dress, like an old-time Italian grandmother. The man wore a shabby suit, too short on the legs and frayed at the cuffs. Anton brought them over to the table and introduced them.

"These are my parents. And this is…" He seemed to realize just then that he didn't even know Jana's name, and for once, he was the one embarrassed. Jana shrugged it off and gave her name. She extended a hand, which the old woman took in her own.

Jana was surprised at the old woman's strength. Her fingers were gnarled, like old tree roots, and her knuckles were knobby. She gripped Jana's palm with a fierceness that frightened the younger woman. She was getting very uncomfortable when Anton finally grasped his mother's arm and pulled her away.

"There, there, Mother. Don't harm the guest."

The old woman nodded. It didn't appear that she could speak any English, but she seemed to get the gist of what Anton was saying, because she released Jana's hand.

The old couple shuffled off to the back room, leaving Anton and Jana alone in the dining room. He sat down in the chair across from her, then thought better of it, and dragged the chair around to her side of the table. Jana's breath quickened as his body drew near. He smelled like musky sweat, a smell that Jana had thought of as the most masculine of scents. Breathing him in was as intoxicating as the wine. She wished that he would kiss her. And then, almost against her will, she kissed him instead.

"Anton," she whispered. He was silent, kissing her back gently at first, but then harder. Jana was shocked at his force; he pressed his mouth against hers as if to bruise it. Somehow, Jana didn't mind.

Nor did she mind when he cupped her face in his hands, tilted it away, and moved his lips down to her neck. It was the best thing Jana had ever felt, a commingling of pleasure and pain, and although she didn't know what was happening to her, she didn't care, either. When the kiss was over, she knew that she was somehow different than before.

She smiled. "Can I have some more wine?" she asked. As she said it, she realized that the wine was the most delicious thing she'd ever tasted, and wondered why she hadn't thought so before. She reached for her near-full glass, and downed it in one swallow. Jana felt like an animal, wild with thirst. "Where's the bottle?" she asked. Anton walked to the back and produced one.

"Welcome to our family," he said, handing her the bottle with a smile.

TOUGH LOVE

Jeremiah Hughes looked at the sun on the horizon of the field. He probably had enough life left to plow two more rows, but he was in a hurry to get back to the house. His wife, Lena, had been sick all day, and he wanted to check on her. Thinking that he'd have to get up extra-early the next day to make up for the lost time, Jeremiah put the mule up and walked toward the house.

Carrie and Thomas were playing in the yard when he got there. Good kids, he thought. He'd told them not to be a bother to their mother that day.

"You two been playing outside, like I asked you?"

"Yes, Pa," they chimed in unison.

"And did you check on her every once in a while to see if she needed anything?"

"I did Pa," said Carrie. "Thomas was lazy, he didn't want to help."

"Good girl, Carrie," Jeremiah said. "Son, I'll talk to you later." The boy bowed his head shamefully, and drew circles in the dirt with his toe.

Jeremiah walked inside and to the back room, where Sarah was sleeping. He went to her bed and put a hand on her forehead, expecting a fever. He drew his hand back in surprise when he realized that her skin was cold as ice.

"Are you cold, darlin'?" he asked with concern.

She didn't respond. She was still sleeping. Jeremiah put an extra blanket over her, kissed her on the cheek, and left her alone to sleep.

He'd expected that Lena would feel better the next day. She was an energetic, hardy woman, and she rarely got ill. But that morning, she was still sound asleep. Jeremiah tried to wake her to see if she needed anything, but he got only a drowsy shake of her head in return.

Jeremiah was useless in the kitchen. He sliced and buttered some bread, leaving it on the counter for the children when they got up. There would be no biscuits today, it seemed. He worked all morning and into the afternoon on an empty stomach. It was a hot day. The air was still, and thick with mosquitoes. His progress was slow, and he couldn't keep his mind off Sarah. At lunchtime, he went back to the house to check on Lena.

She was still asleep. If there had been a doctor nearby, Jeremiah would have sent the children to get him. But the only doctor was in town, nearly half a day's journey away. The only thing that he could do was stay by her side, keep a warm rag on her forehead, and shoo the kids away when they came in to bother her. He fretted about the work that he was losing in the field, but this was more important. There was nothing that he could do about it—he would just have to work even harder for the next few days.

—

That night, Jeremiah fixed dinner as best he could. He knew how to fry bacon, and so he fried a lot of it. He, Thomas, and Carrie had a greasy meal, and the children fell asleep full and happy.

Jeremiah didn't have such an easy time sleeping. He lay in bed next to his wife, almost sick with worry. He worried about the crop, about what he would feed the children the next day, but most of all, he worried about Lena. For years, Lena had been the most constant presence in his life, and in some ways, the most unobtrusive. She kept the house and the family running, day after day, night after night, with no complaint and no need for recognition. Jeremiah was realizing for the first time in a long time that he just would not be able to get along without her.

Sometime during the night, he drifted off. He woke to movement beside him and became instantly alert.

"Lena?"

She looked at him, but didn't speak.

"Lena, are you okay?"

"Hungry," she mumbled. She got up and wandered out into the main room, and Jeremiah followed her. He expected for her to stop in the kitchen, but she didn't. She kept walking, out the door and into the night.

Jeremiah went to the door and called after her, but she kept walking. "Let me be," she called over her shoulder. He felt stung, but tried to brush it off. Maybe she just needs some air after all that time in bed, he thought. He stayed behind and started frying some more bacon, so that she could have something to eat when she got back inside.

But Lena didn't come back inside for a long time.

Jeremiah waited up for hours, eventually eating about half of the bacon himself. He went out looking for her at one point, but when he could not find her, he thought that maybe she had taken another route back to the cabin. She still wasn't there. Jeremiah stayed up for hours, frantic. Sarah came in just before dawn, looking strangely more healthy than she had before.

"Where in the world have you been? I was worried," he said.

"I just needed some air."

"Oh, well. I made you some bacon. It's not hot anymore."

"I'm not hungry," she said.

"Oh."

They both went to bed then, Jeremiah feeling bewildered and hurt, and Lena with a curious, unsettling grin on her face.

—

Jeremiah hoped that after that, things would return to normal. But they did not. Lena kept sleeping days, and she kept going out nights. He let it go for some time, nearly a week. And then one night, he decided to follow her. The sight he saw was one that he knew would never leave him, not until his dying day.

Lena crept out of the bedroom, pausing as she passed the room that held her sleeping children. She peered in the door, and Jeremiah did not like the look on her face. It was a hungry look, half mad. It chilled her husband to the bone. But things just got worse from there.

Once out the front door, her footsteps became faster,

more purposeful. This was no midnight stroll for fresh air; Lena was going somewhere, and she knew what for. She was nearly running by the time she reached the cattle field. Jeremiah tried to stay in shadow at first, but then realized that his wife was too desperate to be cautious. She would not notice him.

Lena jumped the fence and approached one of the cows. What the devil? thought Jeremiah. Lena jumped on the cow's back as if to ride it, and plunged her teeth into its flesh. A shout tore out of Jeremiah's chest. He ran toward his wife, not even sure what he would do when he got there. But when he was near enough to see her face in the moonlight, he knew there was nothing he could do. She looked at him with bloodthirsty eyes, her cheek smeared with hot cow's blood. Jeremiah turned and ran back in the direction of the house. He knew that if he didn't leave Lena there with the cows, then he might be next.

Back at the house, he didn't go into his own room. He went into the room with his children instead, laid a blanket out in front of the door, and lay there. He did not get a wink of sleep all night.

—

The next day, Jeremiah woke up, planted a kiss on the raw, bloodied lips of his wife, and told his children to pack a bag. He knew that it was no longer safe for them there, although he did not tell him that. What he said was that they were going to visit their aunt and uncle in town. The kids shrieked. To them, town meant playing with other children, and trips to the store for hard candy. In no time, they were packed and waiting in the wagon, even before Jeremiah could get it hitched. He hesitated before they left, but eventually decided that it would be safe to leave his wife at home. She had not seen the light of day since this sickness began, and as long as he could get back before nightfall, he should be able to keep her from starting any trouble.

The trip was long and hot, and for Jeremiah, it was filled with sadness and worry. He did not know what would happen next; if he could not figure out a way to cure this disease, it might be awhile before he got to see his children again. He took what small delight he could in their chatter and laughter, although it was bittersweet.

When they got to his brother's house in town, he took Charlie aside and explained, in very vague terms, what he needed. Lena was ill, he said. They needed Charlie and Sue to look after the kids for a while, since she could not. Charlie said that it was fine. He was happy to see his brother, whose fields usually kept him away from town, and asked Jeremiah to at least stay and eat before he headed back. The offer was tempting. Jeremiah was hungry, and the journey had worn him out. But he remembered the crazed look on Lena's face as she bit into that cow, and he knew he had to get back and stop her before she did anything worse.

He thanked Charlie and Sue, hugged the children hard, and went on his way.

When he got back, Lena was still sleeping, thankfully. There was still a little time left to come up with a plan.

Jeremiah sat in a hard chair thinking, but he couldn't think fast enough. Before he could think of what to do, Lena was up, headed for the door in a dreamlike stupor. This time, though, before she left, she stopped and gave Jeremiah a long, deep look, a look that chilled his heart. He didn't dare try to stop her. Instead, he followed her out into the field again, where she felled another of his helpless cows. As Jeremiah watched her, crouched by the fence, he let loose a tide of desperate sobs for the woman he'd loved so long.

—

By the next morning, Jeremiah knew what he had to do. Time was not really an issue; he had all day before Lena would wake up. So he spent some time in the room with her, studying her sleeping face. She looked so calm, so beautiful in sleep. There was no hint of the madness that would overtake her when she woke. He kissed her again and again, unsure if his lips would ever touch her face again.

Although he wanted to stay in that room forever, he forced himself to get up and leave. He filled several buckets of water from the well and put them in Lena's room, along with some meat they'd been storing in the smokehouse.

Then he went and got his tools, and boarded the bedroom door up so tight that she would never be able to break out of it.

After that, Jeremiah went out to the fields to work and take his mind off Lena.

When it was time for him to pack up and go inside for the night, he lingered, deciding to plow one more row before he called it a night. Jeremiah didn't like the thought of what was waiting for him back at the cabin.

Finally night fell, and he could put it off no longer. He unhitched the mule and put it up in the barn, then walked slowly down the path that led to his home. The evening air was still and hot, and as Jeremiah walked through it, he felt as if he were wading in pond water.

He opened the door hoping for quiet, but to his dismay, the moans had already begun. Lena was waking up.

The noises were terrible. Lena screamed and wailed, pounding at the door. Jeremiah could not imagine how much pain she must be in, and the thought of her suffering tore at his heart. Just go outside, he told himself. Don't listen. But he couldn't force himself to leave her there alone. He needed to be there through her suffering, just as they had always been there for each other during hard times. Even if he could not be in the room with her, he did not want Lena to be alone. Several times, he thought of unboarding the door and giving himself over to her. If it was blood she needed, she could have his. The only thing that stopped him was the thought of their children. If he was gone, and she was set loose, what would become of Thomas and Carrie? He could sacrifice himself, but not them. He sat there until the sun rose and her moans subsided.

Jeremiah knew after that night that there could be no cure. Whatever this illness was, it had taken his Lena away for good. For the better part of the day, Jeremiah sat in his chair and cried, for he knew what he had to do.

He took his hatchet and began chopping at the boards that he'd nailed over the door. It was hard work, and it went even slower because Jeremiah dreaded finishing. Finally, though, the hatchet broke through and the door swung open. Lena lay in the bed, white as the sheets beneath her. She was as peaceful as a sleeping child, and Jeremiah almost allowed himself to believe that she was the same woman he'd married, and that everything would be alright.

But he thought again of the children, their children. From this point on, he would have to love Lena through them, through the parts of her beauty and character that shone through in them. Jeremiah raised the hatchet over his sleeping wife. He cried out as he sunk the blade into the heart that for so long had beat only for him, and then for something else, and now, not at all.

HUNTER AND HUNTED

Regina Dears whacked her alarm clock's off button with a little more force than necessary. She'd already pressed snooze three times, and she knew that if she slept any longer, she might miss her appointment with Mario Cruz.

Not that it was a regular appointment, exactly. In fact, Mario Cruz didn't know that Regina was meeting him. Tracking might have been a better word for what she planned to do that morning. Regina was a vampire hunter, and Mario Cruz was her newest assignment.

"What kind of vampire gets coffee at six in the morning?" she muttered to herself as she rolled out of bed. Regina wasn't the best housekeeper; she scanned the piles of clothes on her floor for something inconspicuous to wear, and decided on blue jeans, a black T-shirt, and tennis shoes. She pulled her curly blond hair back into a ponytail and completed the look with a black baseball cap and some large sunglasses. Mario Cruz would not be looking for her, but she might as well go incognito and keep herself from becoming a familiar face.

Putting her car into drive, Regina yawned. It was a popular misconception that sunlight was deadly for all vampires. Actually, they were affected to different degrees, and some of them weren't bothered by it at all. Unfortunately for Regina, who was not a morning person, Mario Cruz was obviously this kind of vampire.

A short drive later, Regina arrived at the café where Landon, her mentor, had told her Cruz had his morning coffee every day at the unholy hour of six a.m. There was a great spot open on the street just in front of the tables, and Regina longed to pull into it. She was a great parallel parker and always eager to show off her skills. But she reminded herself that this was not the time for showing off. She turned into a parking lot in the back of the building, realizing that this approach would give her another advantage as well. She would be able to enter through the back of the café and check out the other customers before they saw her.

Regina was in luck. She'd been briefed about what Mario Cruz would look like, and she spotted him immediately. Although she knew that he'd be about six feet tall, with dark skin and long black hair, Landon hadn't warned her that he would also be gorgeous. Regina took a deep breath, ordered her coffee, and studied Cruz from afar. Not only was he tall, but he was also perfectly built. It was obvious that he spent a good bit of time in the gym. He's a vampire, Reg, she tried to remind herself. It's just as likely that he got those muscles carrying bodies out to his car as he did doing bench presses. Cruz's caramel-colored skin was flawless and smooth, and though she couldn't see his eyes behind the sunglasses, the lips below were full and dark. And, Regina thought with a twinge of jealousy, Cruz's thick black hair, pulled back into a low ponytail, looked healthier and better cared for than her own.

"Mocha latte with skim milk," called out the barista.

Regina took her cup, looked at it, and hesitated. "On second thought, could you put some whipped cream on that?" she asked. After all, she'd saved a bunch of calories by going with the skim milk.

While waiting for the coffee, Regina had debated with herself about whether to sit on the patio near Mario, or inside the shop where she could watch him unobserved. Since her plan for this mission was just to scope the man out and not to make contact, she decided to stay inside and out of sight. Taking a city paper from the rack, she seated herself at a small corner table and proceeded to take mental notes on her target.

Unfortunately, there wasn't much of interest to observe, other than the man himself. He wasn't speaking to or looking at anyone. He was just drinking his coffee alone, his gaze aimed at the sidewalk in front of him. His hands were large, and looked incongruously strong holding the ceramic handle of the delicate mug. As he raised the mug to his lips and sipped his coffee, Regina found her eyes and her thoughts traveling toward his mouth. Those lips, so full, closed gently around the lip of the mug…

Regina shook her head. Snap out of it! she thought. This really would not do. She was supposed to be picking up information about Mario Cruz, and so far, all she had to report back to Landon was that Mario Cruz was one sexy vampire. She was considering stepping her investigation up a notch and taking her coffee out to the patio when

Cruz took his last sip, replaced the mug on the table, and stood up. Regina expected him to produce some car keys, but to her disappointment, he started walking down the sidewalk. Regina hesitated. It would be nearly impossible to follow him in the car if he was on foot, but who knew how far from the coffee shop he might lead her? She didn't want to hoof it all the way across town and then have to turn around and go back to her car.

Oh well, she thought. She would just have to suck it up and go on foot. No one ever told her that being a vampire hunter was going to be convenient. If she could just find out where he lived, then at least she'd have something to report back to Landon at their afternoon briefing.

Mario Cruz proved difficult to follow. It wasn't that Regina had a hard time keeping an eye on him; quite the opposite, in fact. He walked slowly, frequently stopping to window gaze in storefronts or check out the wares of street vendors. Regina was having trouble staying behind him without looking too obvious. She bent to tie her shoe, checked her hair in the reflection of a store window, and pretended to make a call on her cell phone, but she was running out of distractions, and Cruz wasn't making much progress down the block. He must not have anywhere to be today, Regina thought. She looked up and saw him making conversation with a young girl selling pretzels at a stand. Come to think of it, during all of this time, Cruz had seemed more interested in the people on the street than in anything else. Oh my gosh, Regina realized with horror. He's looking for a victim.

Regina instinctively began to march in the direction of the pretzel stand to warn the girl about what kind of man she was flirting with. But she realized that this was not the right time, that Cruz surely wouldn't be planning to strike now, and the girl probably wouldn't believe her anyway. Regina held herself back and waited. After a few minutes Mario Cruz walked on, waving goodbye to the girl and flashing her a sexy grin. Poor thing, Regina thought. She has no idea what that man would like to do to her.

Just then, Regina's cell phone rang. "Dang it!" she muttered. Normally, a cell phone ring on the street wouldn't attract anyone's attention. But Regina had hers programmed to give off one of those shrill, shocking rings like an old-fashioned telephone. She sometimes used it as an alarm clock while napping on the couch. Heads turned in her direction as she rifled through her purse looking for it. Regina cursed herself for not remembering to turn on the silent function. Not sure if Cruz had seen her, she ducked into the open doorway of a storefront. It was too late. She couldn't run the risk of following him any longer if she'd been spotted. She would have to abort the chase for today and begin again the next morning.

—

That afternoon she met Landon at a small bookstore downtown. She was a few minutes early, so she ordered some coffee and took it to a secluded table in the corner of the shop. Trying to relax and shake off the disappointing events of that morning, Regina inhaled the must of dust and old books. It was a scent that always soothed her, reminding her of her father, a professor who'd spent hour after hour in his own personal library at home. A wave of sadness passed over her as she remembered her father. Poor Daddy, she sighed to herself. He had been killed in his home four years before.

Although the police had ruled it a burglary gone wrong, Regina had not been satisfied with that answer. There had been nothing taken from the home, and Regina knew for a fact that some of those old books were worth lots of money. She'd spent months researching the case on her own and was especially fixated on the fact that two small holes had been found on her father's neck.The police blamed the family cat, but Regina had spoken to the mortician, a quiet, scared-looking woman who had told her in strictest confidence that there was something strange about the body. When the mortician had gone to drain the blood, there had been almost none left to drain.

From there, Regina's investigations had led her to Landon, who had written several books on the subject of vampires. Although most of the world viewed him as a leading scholar in a somewhat disreputable field, only Regina and a handful of others knew that he coordinated the efforts of those dedicated to hunting and getting rid of vampires. Inspired by the loss of her father, Regina had signed on as a vampire hunter, accepting Landon's warnings that the job would be dangerous, irregular, and thankless. If ever she started to regret the decision she'd made, she thought again about her father tucked away in the dusty library that gave him so much joy, harming no one, and Regina knew that she'd make the same decision all over again.

Just then, the door of the bookstore opened, breaking into Regina's reverie. Landon walked in looking every bit the academic that he was in his public life. He wore small round glasses, a tweed coat with leather patches at the elbow, and carried a briefcase on a strap over his shoulder. Regina smiled when she saw him, and stood to greet him. She loved Landon like a second father.

He sat down, and they exchanged some small talk. Landon brought Regina up to date on his latest book, and she listened with interest. Finally, they got around to the subject of Mario Cruz.

Regina buried her face in her hands and gave a huge sigh. "I blew it, Landon," she said. "My cell phone went off, and I think that he might have seen me. I didn't even get to find out where he lives."

Landon looked disappointed, but did his best to reassure Regina. "Now, don't worry. He's not going to get away from us that easy. You'll just have to try again tomorrow."

Regina went on to tell him about how she thought Cruz might be looking for his next victim. She mentioned the pretzel girl, and Landon confirmed that she'd done the right thing by hanging back. He agreed that Mario was probably looking for prey. According to his source, an anonymous tip who hadn't given much else in the way of information, that was how Landon liked to operate. He relied on his good looks and sex appeal to get him close to his prey, so his victims were normally women. "Go back to the coffee shop tomorrow and see if you can keep an eye on him. But don't blow your cover just yet. Not until you absolutely have to."

—

Regina woke up the next day with renewed commitment to the hunt. She was determined to find out all she could about Mario Cruz that morning, if for no other reason than to hurry toward the day when she could stop getting up at 5:30 a.m. She dressed in an outfit similar to the one she'd worn the day before and pulled her hair back beneath a different baseball cap. She looked in the mirror. "Pretty unremarkable," she said with a self-satisfied nod. It was exactly the effect she was hoping to achieve.

Pulling into the café again, Regina caught a sideways look at Mario Cruz. He was sitting at the same table as yesterday, reading a paper and sipping his coffee. Regina stepped inside and made her order—whole milk this time, and whipped cream, too. She deserved it for getting up this early two days in a row. She took a seat—a different one, but still toward the back of the café, and waited.

Mario took his time with his coffee that day. Regina pretended to read the paper but noticed that from behind his sunglasses, his gaze followed any young woman or girl who happened to pass on the sidewalk in front of the café. He's really looking for someone. He must be getting hungry.

A plan began to form in Regina's mind. It wasn't something that Landon would like—he would say it was too risky. Landon liked to do things by the book: track the vampire, get to know his patterns and habits, and then strike when he's not expecting it, when he's resting. But Regina looked again at the way that Cruz scanned the sidewalk. He would soon find another victim. She thought of the pretzel girl, how young she'd looked, and how unaware of what she was dealing with. Regina had to try to stop him. She pulled a small compact out of her purse, then took her hair out of its ponytail and tried to fluff some volume into it. She applied a coat of shiny gloss to her lips. There was nothing she could do about her outfit, but she hade a feeling that Cruz wasn't going to be too picky about whom he struck up a conversation with at this point. Regina took her coffee mug and paper outside and sat down at a table close to his.

Regina pretended to read the paper. It wasn't long at all before Cruz was staring at her. Her hunch had been right. Cruz was on the prowl.

"Anything good in there?" he asked. It was a pretty lame attempt at conversation, Regina noted, since he had a copy of the same paper in front of him. But she kept the thought to herself. Cruz liked to lure his prey by flirting, and so Regina would flirt back.

"A few good concerts coming to town. Do you like music?"

Cruz flashed her a certain smile, and Regina had to remind herself again that the man was a killer. That smile could melt icecaps—it was easy to see how women could fall so easily into his trap. "I love music," he said. "All kinds." Regina smiled and went back to pretending to read. She was confident that he would take the initiative from here, and she didn't want to seem overeager. After all, he was supposed to be hunting her, not the other way around.

"Are you waiting for someone?" he asked.

"Just enjoying the day."

"It's going to be a beautiful one," he said. "I can feel it already."

"What about you? Are you waiting for somebody?"

"Just enjoying the day. What do you say I join you? We could enjoy the day together."

Perfect. He was falling right into her plan. "Well, sure. I guess that'd be alright." Regina held her breath as Cruz moved his coffee over to her table. Landon would absolutely kill her if he knew what she was up to.

"My name is Mario," he said. He held out a strong hand across the table.

"Regina," she said, taking his hand. His skin was hot and smooth, and he had a strong grip. He held on to her palm longer than he needed to, rubbing his thumb up and down for a moment before releasing it. Regina's breath quickened. Mario Cruz certainly was a fast mover. And pretty sure of himself.

"So, Mario, what do you do?"

He laughed. "Oh, a little of this, a little of that. Each day brings what it will." He leaned back in his chair and looked up toward the cloudless sky. "For example, today, I came to get some coffee. I read the paper. I met a beautiful woman. Tomorrow, who knows."

"I mean, what do you do for a living?"

"I know what you mean. But let's not talk business today."

"Okay. If you say so." Regina could see how this answer might be appealing to some women. They might think that he was mysterious or dangerous. They wouldn't know the half of it.

Regina had been prepared to say that she was in retail, but she was relieved not to have to lie about her own job. She changed the subject.

"Do you come here a lot?"

"Every day. Best coffee in town." They sat for a while in silence. Cruz had removed his sunglasses and was staring at Regina with chocolate-colored eyes. A hint of a smile played at the corners of his lips, and Regina noticed that he had dimples. Unusual for a vampire. She tried to keep her thoughts professional. Cruz's warm eyes, which crossed her face slowly and settled around the area of her mouth, were not helping much.

They finished their coffee around the same time. "So, what do you say, Regina? Would you like to go for a walk with me?"

She pretended to hesitate. "Where would we go?"

"You're a very practical-minded person, aren't you?"

"I guess I am."

"Well, you should try being impulsive for a change. Let's take a walk. See where the road takes us."

Regina agreed, and they set off. Mario walked in the same direction that he'd gone the day before. That's right, Regina thought. Take me home. Someplace private. She just hoped that when they finally got there, she would prove to be a more skillful opponent than he anticipated.

The day was turning warm, and they walked slowly in the heat. But Cruz didn't dally the way that he had the previous day, which confirmed Regina's suspicion that he'd been hunting a victim. The same girl was working at the pretzel vendor when they passed, and Regina noticed that she gave Mario a stung look. He caught her glance, and Regina saw him smile and shrug. The girl smiled back, a pouty kind of smile that said she wouldn't be hard to win back over. I've got to get him today, before he has time to get to her or someone like her, thought Regina. An image of her father surged up in her mind and strengthened her.

"So, you said you like music?" Cruz asked.

"Of course."

"Have you ever heard music played on a record player?"

Regina had. Her father had a turntable in his library, and they used to sit in there and listen to classical records on long Sunday afternoons. It was how she'd learned to love music. But Regina was working out a strategy, and so she played naïve.

"No, never. Those old-fashioned things? I didn't know they even still made them."

"Oh, yes. You don't know what you're missing. It adds a whole new dimension to the music. Would you like to hear one?"

Her heart thumped harder. Not trusting herself to speak, Regina nodded."Where would we find something like that?"

"I have one. At my apartment." Cruz reached out and brushed his fingertips across the back of Regina's hand as if he wanted to hold her hand. Not being such a fast mover herself, she instinctively jerked away, but not before his touch could send a sharp chill up her spine. Regina was disturbed to realize that it wasn't entirely a shiver of fear; there had been something pleasurable in it, too. What am I getting myself into? she wondered. When she was hunting vampires, she made it a point to be on top of her game, 100 percent focused. This was proving to be extremely hard to do in the presence of someone who looked like Mario Cruz.

"I'm sorry," she said to Mario, who was looking at her with concern on his face. "It's just…"

"No, do not apologize. I'm the one who should apologize. I should not be so pushy. You are just wanting to listen to some music, and that is what we will do. You will still come, won't you?"

Regina didn't point out that she hadn't actually agreed to go with him to his apartment. "I don't know," she said. Of course, she knew that she would go. It would be the only way to get him alone. But it seemed that the more she played hard to get, the harder Mario was trying to reel her in. If she could keep him in the dark about wanting to go up to the apartment, maybe she would be at an advantage over him.

"Come on. Please? I will be a good boy, cross my heart."

"Well, okay, I guess. But we're just going to listen to music, right?"

"I promise."

"Okay."

In a few more minutes, they came to a stop in front of a small duplex. "This is it. Home sweet home." Mario pulled a key and opened the door. Inside, the apartment was small but sophisticated. The furniture was made of dark, rich wood, and there were antique rugs covering portions of the hardwood floor. The curtains were drawn, and low light emanated from a few well-placed lamps.

"This is very nice," said Regina. She wondered about Mario's source of income, but didn't want to revisit the subject of work.

"Have a seat. I'll get us something to drink. What'll you have? Wine, whiskey?"

Regina giggled nervously. "It's a little early for me. Just some water, please." Mario looked disappointed, but he walked into the kitchen and returned with a glass of ice water.

"Now, I promised you music." He walked to a large wooden cabinet and lifted the top up to reveal a turntable. He bent over to thumb through a crate of records, giving Regina a good view of him in his jeans from behind. She bit her lip and tried not to look. Stay focused, she told herself.

"Do you have a bathroom?" she asked. Mario pointed the way, and Regina went, taking her purse along with her. Once inside she locked the door and started rummaging through her purse. She hadn't seen anything in Mario's apartment she could use for a weapon, and she always kept some supplies with her in any case. She took out a palm-sized wooden spike and tucked it into the waistband of her jeans. She flushed the toilet for show and ran her hands beneath the faucet for a moment, collecting her thoughts. It would be time soon. She thought again of Mario bending over in those jeans, and she wondered if she shouldn't give him just one little kiss before she put him down forever. Jeez, snap out of it! she told herself, shaking her head.

When she got back into the main room, there was music coming from the speakers. Mario had chosen a jazzy sounding album that didn't sound familiar to Regina. "Do you like it?" he asked.

She nodded and headed back to sit down on the couch again, but he reached out and touched her arm as she walked by. This time, she didn't flinch.

"How about a little dance?" he asked, quickly adding, "No pressure. You don't have to dance if you don't want to."

Regina realized that this might be a perfect opportunity to get close to him. She played shy. "Well, I don't know…"

"Oh, come on." His grip closed gently around her arm and he pulled her in to him. He smelled of sandalwood—deep, rich, and sexy, and Regina reminded herself not to inhale too deeply. She told herself to stay alert.

Mario put his other hand on her back and began moving his hips in time to the music. Regina did the same. Outside, she appeared relaxed, but inside, her nerves were a sizzling blaze of excitement, fear, and lust. She'd never felt like this with a vampire before. She nearly panicked wondering if it would interfere with her performance. She had to get this right. After all, Landon didn't even know where this guy lived.

Mario's hands slid down, resting for a moment on the small of Regina's back, and then moving onto her hips. He stepped in a little closer to her, their faces nearly touching. One little kiss, she thought. What would it hurt?

The thought was ridiculous enough to bring Regina back to her senses. What was she thinking? This guy was good. If he could nearly seduce someone who knew he was a vampire, the control he'd have over unsuspecting victims must be incredible. Regina called up the image of her father's face. Immediately, her feelings turned hard. Her resolve came back.

"Ouch!" she said, crouching down to the floor. The move was meant to catch Mario off guard, and it worked. It gave Regina the chance to draw the stake out from her waistband, and when Mario bent down to see what was the matter, she knocked him off-balance. He lay on his back on the ground, and before he could struggle up again, she threw her weight at him, plunging the stake into his chest.

Mario's face crumpled into astonished horror. He tried to speak, but no words came out. "I know who you are," she said. "And I've heard music on a record player before." She took one long look at his beautiful face, knowing that it would never be seen by anyone again. Within moments, Mario Cruz's perfect body had been replaced by a pile of ashes.

"What a shame," said Regina as she stepped over the pile on her way to the door.

NEIGHBORS

Madeline Lagrange sat on her bed looking out of the window at the rainy afternoon. She sighed deeply, slammed shut the book on her lap, and banged her head into the wall behind her. But pouting was somewhat less satisfying when there was no one around to witness it. She opened the book again.

Madeline should have been looking forward to summer vacation, only a week away, but instead she was dreading it. This was Madeline's senior year of high school, and this summer would have been her last chance to relax and spend quality time with her friends before they all left for college. But one night of trouble had ruined everything for Madeline—her parents had caught her trying to sneak back into the house hours after curfew, and they had decided that her punishment would be to spend the summer months living with her grandmother who had an old plantation house out in Hartville, which Madeline referred to as "the middle of nowhere."

"Madeline, come down to dinner honey," called her mother.

Madeline stomped toward the stairs. "Don't call me 'honey,' Mother."

Mrs. Lagrange rolled her eyes. "Okay. Excuse me, Madeline," she said. Mrs. Lagrange had raised three children, the youngest of whom was Madeline, and she no longer got her feathers ruffled by sulky behavior. Madeline had messed up, and she was just going to have to accept her punishment. There was no amount of petulance that would change Mr. and Mrs. Lagrange's minds about that.

Madeline was silent all through dinner, refusing even to give one-word answers to her parents' questions about how school was that day. Finally they stopped even trying to include her in the conversation and went about discussing work and other matters with each other. Mr. Lagrange was right in the middle of a story about one of his new employees when Madeline burst into a new tantrum.

"WHY?" she sang out in a shrill voice. "Why do I have to go to Grandma's?"

"You know exactly why," her mother answered. "You broke the rules. We've agreed to let you go to your graduation party, but after that, it's off to Hartville."

"Hartville! What kind of place is it anyway, with a name like that? I'll bet there's not a mall. I'll bet there's not even a telephone!"

"Madeline, stop it," said Mr. Lagrange. "You sound like a child. You're about to graduate from high school. Just accept the consequences of your actions, and get on with it. We're sorry that you aren't looking forward to this, but we're tired of hearing about it. And who knows, you might even decide that Hartville's more interesting than you think."

"I doubt it," Madeline whined.

She would soon find out.

—

The last week of school passed quickly. Madeline was so busy studying for exams, passing her yearbook around to be signed, and thinking about graduation that she barely had time to dread going to Hartville. It wasn't until the graduation party at her friend Kristin's house that she finally broke down. Some of the girls were sitting out by the edge of Kristin's pool, dipping their feet in, and they started talking about their plans for the summer. Kristin was going to be working at the ice cream shop, Lindsay would be taking a course for college credit, and Rachel was just going to relax and enjoy her last few months of sleeping late before classes started. An awkward silence followed as the other girls looked at Madeline.

"We're going to miss you so much!" said Rachel at last, and Madeline burst into tears as the other girls gathered in a hug around her.

—

The morning after the party, Mrs. Lagrange let Madeline sleep a little late, but not late enough. She was still wrapped up in the covers when her mother knocked and stuck her head in the door.

"Come on, honey. We need to leave here in a couple of hours."

Madeline groaned. Her mother didn't know it, but she hadn't even finished packing yet. She'd been hoping, right up until that moment, that her parents would somehow let her off the hook. It didn't look like that was going to happen. Madeline rolled out of bed and threw all of her jeans and most of her T-shirts into the huge duffel bag she'd used last year at summer camp. She left behind her curling iron, her dresses and high heels, and most of her makeup. After all, Madeline didn't imagine herself spending the summer trying to impress her Grandmother Craine.

—

"Comfy back there?" Mr. Lagrange asked Madeline from the front seat of the car. Against her protests, both of her parents had decided to ride along on the three-hour trip to Hartville. Although she'd told them they didn't both need to go, Madeline was secretly glad that they had. As they got closer to Hartville, she started to suspect that she might actually miss them a little, despite how mad she still was.

They drove out of town, the buildings getting shabbier and farther apart as they went. Through small towns with single stoplights, and miles and miles of pasture. The Lagranges didn't often travel far beyond their suburb and the adjacent city, so even though they lived in a fairly rural state, Madeline wasn't used to seeing much scenery like this. Although she would never say it out loud to her parents, she found herself gazing at the green fields and empty sky and thinking that it was actually very pretty. It was no mall, of course…

At some point, Madeline dozed off. She was awakened by the car's bouncing motion, which knocked her head against the padded seat. Opening her eyes, Madeline was confused at first, and she had to think backwards to figure out where she was. The van bumped along a red clay road lined on either side with thick green trees. Madeline felt like she'd never seen so much green in her whole life.

"Where are we?" she asked.

"Almost there. You slept for a while," said Mrs. Lagrange. "Mother lives just down this road."

It had been years since Madeline had gone to visit her grandmother, Eleanor Craine. The Lagranges saw her several times a year, but it was usually at their own house. Even though she was well into her seventies, Eleanor still had perfect vision and clarity of mind. She insisted that she was very capable of making the three-hour drive by herself on holidays, and so far, she'd never done anything to contradict that claim. She always showed up at the Lagrange's door on time, carrying presents and a tin of homemade cinnamon rolls. If the Lagranges ever offered to come visit at her house, she made some excuse, saying that her house was too musty and old, or too far out of the way for everyone in the family to drive. They suspected that she just didn't like cleaning the place up for company, and they had been very surprised when she'd agreed to let Madeline come and stay for the summer.

After about a mile on the dirt road, the forest gave way, and the Lagranges found themselves in a wide clearing of yard. At the back of the lot was Eleanor's house, a rambling old plantation-style mansion. Huge white columns stretched up to support an upper balcony threaded with ivy. Below was a front porch that ran the length of the house. There were several rocking chairs on the porch, along with some small wicker footrests. Madeline was stunned. Her recollection of the place was vague and dreamlike, but she had not remembered it being nearly so big.

"Grandmother lives here all by herself?" asked Madeline. She knew that was the case, but she was amazed that a woman in her seventies could keep up such a big place.

"As far as we know."

"I wonder what she does around here. It's got to get boring. Are there any neighbors?"

"Not for miles."

"Jeez," Madeline said under her breath. "What in the world am I going to do all summer long?"

"I'm sure you and your grandmother will find plenty of things to keep you busy. And you haven't seen her in a while. You'll have lots of catching up to do."

"Great. Fantastic," Madeline said, thinking, It's going to be one long summer.

Eleanor came out onto the porch as the Lagranges were unloading Madeline's things from the car. She was a petite woman, barely five feet tall and probably weighing ninety pounds, but she carried herself with such poise and strength that she seemed larger than she actually was. She was dressed neatly in slacks and a button-down shirt with a string of pearls at her neck. Her silver hair was pulled back into a low bun at the nape of her neck. At seventy-three, Eleanor's posture was still rod-straight, and there was nothing frail about her arms as they encircled Madeline in a tight hug.

"Good lord, child. You've grown up since Christmas!"

Madeline smiled. "It's great to see you, Grandma."

The family hauled Madeline's things inside. Eleanor insisted on carrying one of the bags, despite Mr. Lagrange's protests.

Once they were all inside Eleanor offered them lemonade, which they accepted. The family took their drinks out onto the porch and sat there for a while, talking and rocking in the chairs, catching up on one another's lives. The Lagranges hadn't planned on staying for dinner, and before long it was time for them to go. As they hugged their daughter tight, Madeline noticed tears in her mother's eyes. For a split second she thought, Good. I hope she's sorry for making me stay here all summer. I hope she misses me a lot. But these thoughts faded when she realized that she had tears in her own eyes and that she was probably going to miss her parents as much as they would miss her.

Eleanor and Madeline waved from the porch as Mr. and Mrs. Lagrange's car drove off, kicking up a red cloud of dust from the road.

"Well," said Eleanor, "Looks like it's just you and me. Cheer up, dear. Let's make you something to eat." She put an arm around her granddaughter's shoulder and led her inside to the spacious kitchen.

As Eleanor cooked, Madeline looked on from her barstool at the high kitchen counter. They chatted steadily as delicious smells began to rise from the pots and pans. When they had both stuffed themselves on creamed corn, turnip greens seasoned with pork fat, cornbread, black-eyed peas, and sliced ham, Madeline found that she could hardly keep her eyes open.

"Why don't you call it a night, honey?" suggested Eleanor. "You've had a long day."

Madeline agreed. She kissed her grandmother on the cheek and thanked her for dinner. She was on her way up the stairs when the old woman called out to her. "Madeline?"

"Yes?"

Eleanor hesitated for a moment. "I don't want to make you nervous, but be sure to sleep with your windows closed tonight. We've had a small problem with—bats. I believe that I've taken care of it, but if you do see one, then run out of the room and yell for me as loud as you can. Alright?"

Madeline had stopped in her tracks. "Okay. If you say so," she replied. As she continued up the steps, she suppressed a shiver. What a creepy thing to tell me right before I go to sleep, she thought. Oh well. Maybe she's just going senile. I haven't seen any bats.

But she still made sure that the windows were shut tight before crawling into the creaky, oversized bed.

—

The next morning, Madeline thought back on the bat comment as if it were a dream. She'd been so tired, maybe she'd misheard Eleanor. She decided to ask about it later.

It was nearly eleven o'clock when she padded down the stairs, and Eleanor was not in the kitchen or on the porch. Madeline finally found her out back in the garden, pulling up weeds with vigor, as if she were in the best shape of her life.

"I'm impressed, Grandma," she said.

Eleanor turned around with a jump, wielding the garden trowel before her like a dagger, her face sheet-white and angry. It only took her a second to recover, but Madeline had seen the expression and was unsettled. "I'm sorry. I didn't mean to scare you."

Eleanor waved away her apology. "No, I'm the one who's sorry, child. I didn't mean to turn on you like that. You just startled me! A person gets used to living alone and it gets to be quite a shock to hear another voice come out of nowhere."

Madeline gave a shaky smile. "It's okay. I understand. Can I help you out here?" For the rest of the afternoon they worked together in the garden. Madeline considered asking about the bats, but it didn't seem like a good time.

—

Later on, Eleanor said that she needed a nap and told Madeline to entertain herself for a few hours. The girl wandered around the house for a while looking for something to do. There was no television. The old radio only picked up two channels, neither of which Madeline wanted to listen to. She finally came across a stack of paperback mystery novels and took one of them out onto the porch with a glass of lemonade.

Sitting back in one of the old rockers and putting her feet up on the table, Madeline sighed. She opened the paperback in her lap. Two whole months of this. Better get used to it, she thought. She read for a while, but the novel didn't grab her attention. She leaned back in the chair and looked out at the forest and at the dirt road winding through it. She was wondering what her friends were doing at that moment. Probably sitting by the pool, gossiping, laughing…

At that moment, a movement on the road caught Madeline's eye. She jerked her head up from its relaxed position and stared. Standing in the middle of the road was a young man about Madeline's age. He was tall and thin with wavy black hair that fell long on his ears and forehead. Even though he was nearly thirty feet away, Madeline could feel the weight of his eyes on her. She could hardly breathe. The man's clothes looked old-fashioned; he was wearing trousers, a white shirt with suspenders over it, and a dark hat pushed down onto his head. He looked like something out of an antique family photo album. Madeline wondered if her eyes were playing tricks on her. She blinked, and he was gone.

I've got to get out of this heat, she thought. Forgetting to gather up the lemonade glass and the novel, she walked inside in a daze and went to her bedroom, where she slept until the rich smells of dinner woke her.

—

"Did you sleep well?" Eleanor asked when her granddaughter finally woke up and went downstairs.

Madeline nodded but didn't say anything. She walked over to the stove and stirred the beef stew that her grandmother was simmering.

"Grandma, do you have any neighbors around here?"

Eleanor turned sharply. "No. What makes you ask that?"

Madeline was caught a little off-guard. Her grandmother's expression resembled the same startled one she'd worn this morning in the garden. "It's nothing. I was probably just imagining things."

"What kind of things?" Eleanor pushed.

"Well, earlier today I thought that I saw a guy standing out on the road. He was dressed really old-timey. But I didn't see where he came from, and when I looked again, he was gone. So I probably just imagined it. Right?"

Eleanor was staring straight at Madeline but she didn't answer. "Grandma? Don't you think it was a daydream?"

When Eleanor finally did speak, it was in a harsh tone that Madeline had never heard her use before. It frightened the girl. "No. It probably wasn't a daydream. There are some very unsavory characters that come into these woods sometimes. Probably moonshiners or poachers. Very dangerous types. If you ever see him again, come and get me immediately. Don't you dare talk to him, or to anyone like him."

After the speech, Eleanor closed her eyes and put her hand to her head. "I'm not feeling very well. You eat what you like, then put the stew away. I'm going to bed. Remember what I said about the bats, and keep your window shut." With that, she marched out of the kitchen. Madeline stood in place, stunned, listening to her grandmother's hard footsteps ascending the stairs.

—

Madeline found that she didn't have much of an appetite either that night. She let the stew cool, transferred it into a plastic container, and refrigerated it. Then she went to bed, making sure that the windows were shut. She had nearly drifted off to sleep when she heard footsteps in the hallway. The front door creaked open and then shut. Madeline crawled from her bed and went to the window. She was shocked to see her grandmother crossing the yard in only her white nightgown and a cardigan sweater. Worried, she nearly called out to the old woman, but she remembered her grandmother's harsh voice that evening and held her tongue. Whatever Eleanor was doing out there, she obviously didn't want Madeline to know about. Still, curiosity got the better of her. This is definitely the most excitement I'm going to have in this house all summer, and I don't want to miss it, she thought as she pulled on her robe and slipped into her tennis shoes. Seconds later she was out the door, walking toward the woods in the spot that her grandmother had entered them.

The trees formed a canopy that was nearly black beneath. Madeline had to wait for her eyes to adjust before continuing. When she walked on, it was with quiet, careful steps. If she got caught she'd just say that she saw Eleanor going into the woods and came after her, but for some reason she knew that she didn't want to be caught.

Madeline began to hear voices and she stopped in her tracks. Stepping backward a little, she saw the white of her grandmother's nightgown in a small clearing in the woods. The old woman wasn't alone. With her were several other people—a middle-aged man and woman, a small child, and the young man that she'd seen earlier.

"How dare you?" Eleanor was saying. "We had an agreement!"

"The agreement still stands," replied the older man,

who seemed to be the father of the group. "None of us has broken it."

"Maybe not, but you've gotten uncomfortably close to it. My granddaughter saw him today. Your Edward." She pointed at the young man, whose head was bowed in shame.

"I'm sorry," he stuttered. "I didn't mean to go so close. But there was a girl. This girl. She was—I'm sorry. I had to go closer."

"You stay away from my granddaughter. Or else you'll all be sorry."

"It will not happen again," assured the father. "You have my word."

The young man was still looking downward. His lips were moving as if in prayer. Madeline heard him whisper the words, "She was so beautiful. I had to be closer."

Finished with her business, Grandmother Eleanor spun on her heel and began walking briskly back toward the house. Madeline backed further from the path, held her breath, and closed her eyes. She felt her grandmother passing no more than three feet in front of her, but lost in fury, the old woman hadn't seen her. When Madeline opened her eyes though, she realized that someone else had.

Edward was staring at her through the trees. Their eyes locked and Madeline felt that she might never be able to look away. His dark hair was tousled around his face. His stare was so intense, so sorrowful, that Madeline wanted to run to him. Around Edward, his family argued and spat orders. He did not seem to hear them.

"Edward!" shouted the father. The young man broke the gaze, and Madeline ran.

—

Madeline didn't sleep at all that night. Strange feelings stirred in her chest and kept her awake. She'd had boyfriends before; she'd had dates and crushes, and she thought that she'd even been in love once. Until now. This was like nothing she'd ever felt, and it made every boy in her past seem like just that: a boy. This Edward, she thought, was going to be someone important to her. She knew that. She had to have him.

Eleanor slept late after her trip to the woods, so Madeline was alone when she woke at dawn and went out to sit on the porch. She sat in the rocking chair and stared at the spot where she had entered the woods, the spot that had changed her. She felt that she had gone into the woods as one person and emerged as another. She stared at it for what felt like hours.

Edward emerged like a ghost, slowly at first and then faster, seeming to glide across the ground as he came toward her. His gait was so graceful, so smooth. Madeline, not afraid at all, ran to meet him.

He spoke before she could. "You're just beautiful," he said. "I had to come and tell you." Madeline giggled out of nervousness. Edward went on. "I won't see you again, but I just had to tell you. That's all." With that he turned to leave.

"Wait," she called. "Why are you going? Please stay."

"No. I won't. Believe me, I will not see you again. I just had to get closer to you, just this once." Madeline reached out to grab his sleeve but he pulled out of her grasp and ran back to the woods, not even looking over his shoulder.

Madeline stood in that spot awhile longer and then turned and walked up to the house.

—

The mood around the house that day was filled with tension between Madeline and Eleanor. Each had a secret. Each wondered how much the other knew. Neither knew how to begin. But that afternoon as they were cleaning up the dishes from lunch, the words came tumbling out of both women at the same time.

"Madeline, we need to…"

"Grandma, who were those…"

Both smiled, and Eleanor went on. "Fix yourself a glass of tea. Let's go into the sitting room and chat."

The two of them sat at either ends of the soft couch. Eleanor took a deep breath and began. "Madeline, I have lived in this house for twenty years. I moved in just after my husband died and my children moved on to have their own lives. This house has been something very special to me. It has kept me going through times when I might otherwise have broken down."

Madeline nodded. She didn't really know where her grandmother was going with all of this.

"As with every home, there are some aspects that are less pleasing than others. For example, a person might live in a nice house on a road that's too busy. Or a person might have a beautiful view of the mountains but live in a tiny shack."

Madeline was still confused but went along with this, eager to put her grandmother in a good mood for when it was her turn to ask the questions. "Right. Like our house is in a good location, but Mom always says it doesn't have enough windows," she offered.

"Exactly. And sometimes you move into a place where everything seems perfect, but then you find out a thing or two about the neighbors."

"Yes?" Madeline nodded eagerly. This was just where she wanted the conversation to go.

"My neighbors, for example. Oh, yes," she said waving her hand. "I have neighbors. Nobody knows it. They're not the kind of neighbors one brags about. But they have deep roots on this property. They've been here much longer than I have."

Feigning ignorance, Madeline asked, "Is the man I saw yesterday one of your neighbors?" Eleanor nodded. "Well, he looked alright to me. Why wouldn't you want to brag about him?"

There was a long pause. "That man is not what you think. Tell me, do you ever read horror stories?"

"Grandma, please. Don't change the subject!"

"Unfortunately, I'm not changing the subject. Have you ever heard of what's called a vampire?"

"Um, yeah. Of course. What does that have to do with this?"

Eleanor looked grave. All of a sudden, things started clicking into place for Madeline. The bats. The closed windows. The family awake in the middle of the night.

"Grandma, what are you saying?"

"I believe that you already know. I share this property with a family of vampires. The young man that you saw yesterday was one of them."

Madeline felt sure that her grandmother was losing her mind. But then, it made everything else make sense.

Eleanor went on. "This family, they have a special ability. They are able to transform themselves into bats at will. They live in these woods, and when they need to feed, they fly into some town or another by night. Then they transform, do what they need to, and change again. They fly back here as bats. They disappear. They are untraceable. You and I are probably the only people in the world who know that they exist."

"But why would you live near them? Why wouldn't you just move?"

"Like I said. This place is perfect for me. And we've come to an agreement."

"What kind of agreement?"

"They leave me alone, along with everyone else who comes into my house, and I let them live."

A laugh escaped Madeline. She'd seen television shows about vampire hunters—young, fit women skilled in martial arts. Her grandmother hardly fit the bill.

Eleanor sat up straight and put on a hurt expression, but there was a tiny smile on her lips. "Why, don't you think I am capable?" she asked.

"It's not that, Grandma."

"They tried to get to me, once. My first night in this house. One of them, the grandfather, flew in through my open window. But I'm a good shot. I splattered him all over the wall before he had a chance to turn back into a man. The next day they sent a representative over and we struck up our deal."

"Oh," Madeline said, because she didn't know what else to say.

"I am telling you this for a reason. I will not live forever, as you know. Your parents will never leave those suburbs they've chosen to live in. But you, Madeline. I think that one day you might enjoy this house."

"Me?"

"Yes. I plan to leave it to you. The house, the land, everything. You may do with it as you wish, but it will be yours. The deal that I made was sealed in blood, the blood of that family's grandfather. It will be passed along to you as well. You will be safe. Unless, of course, you go near them."

"What do you mean?"

"I mean, you must stay away from them, and they will stay away from you. Deal or no deal, they are what they are. They would not be able to resist the temptation for long. They would drain your blood, Madeline. They would make you one of them if you stayed too long."

Madeline rested her head against the couch and closed her eyes, trying to take this all in.

And then her grandmother added, "And if you go near that boy again this summer, I'll shoot him, too."

—

The years passed. Madeline grew up. Although she'd sworn that she would never return to Hartville after that summer, when Eleanor died in Madeline's twenty-fifth year, she felt the old pull of those woods calling her home. She took the house and moved in there. By this time, she had a husband and a small child.

Madeline wondered sometimes about Edward, the young man in the woods. She thought that maybe she had dreamed him up. She would look at her own husband, whom she loved dearly, and decide that yes, she must have dreamed it. No real man could be as perfect as Edward had been.

Then one day as she was watering the potted plants on the front porch, Madeline looked up and saw him— Edward, standing at the same place on the road that she had first seen him. He was no older than he had been that summer, and he was no less perfect. Madeline's heart lurched within her. They locked eyes for what seemed like an eternity, and then Edward was gone. This time, Madeline did not fail to notice the tiny black speck, a bat, flapping its wings against the enormous sky.

A DAY AT THE HOSPITAL

Sitting in his car in the parking lot, Greg Vines stared in the direction of the hospital, watching the people enter and leave. Nervous families carrying balloons and bunches of flowers, hurried nurses on their way back from lunch, and eager volunteers carrying coloring books, cookies, anything that might cheer up the sick children inside. These were good people, Greg thought. He took a deep breath, trying to quell the terrible hunger that gnawed almost constantly at his belly. Greg told himself again that he would not give in to it. He turned off the ignition, locked the door of his beaten up old Honda, and walked toward the hospital.

For years, Greg had been fighting against the one thing that he truly hated about himself—the fact that he was a vampire. He had been bitten by a lover, a one-night fling that he'd met at a book signing, and had awakened the next morning to find that his usual morning hunger for eggs and toast had been replaced by an undeniable craving for human blood.

Greg had been horrified. A professional student of philosophy, he considered himself a pacifist, opposed to the taking of human life. And what's more, he'd been a vegetarian for the past ten years. In a haze, he had run to the corner market and bought the biggest steak that they sold. He took it home and ate it raw. Since that moment, Greg had lived a constant struggle between his long-held beliefs and his newly acquired physiological needs. He'd had no choice but to give up being a vegetarian. He'd become a regular customer at the local pet store, where he bought live mice by the dozen, then took them home, bit their heads off, and drained them like little push-up pops. The people at the pet store thought that he raised pythons.

Volunteering at the hospital was one way that Greg maintained his self-control and kept from eating actual humans. The people who volunteered with him tended to be genuinely good people—charitable, kind, and sincere. If he surrounded himself with people like that on a regular basis, he felt even guiltier at the thought of eating the living, and he was able to consign himself to the diet of white mice for a little bit longer.

Today was one of those days. He'd woken up starving, repulsed by the thought of picking white fur from his teeth after breakfast, and he'd longed for nothing more than to sink his teeth into the warm flesh of a pretty, unsuspecting neck. So, off to the hospital he went.

At the sign-in desk inside, Greg couldn't help but notice a beautiful young woman who seemed to be having some trouble with the receptionist.

"No," she said, "I'm supposed to be here. I'm volunteering today."

"I'm sorry, ma'am. I don't have you on the list."

Greg approached them. After having volunteered for

nearly two years, he was on friendly terms with Gina, the receptionist. "Hi Gina," he said. "I couldn't help but overhear. Is there a problem?"

"This young lady says she's supposed to volunteer, but she's not on the list." Gina rolled her eyes at him. Gina was jaded.

The other woman looked at him, too, but with a helpless, desperate expression on her clear face. Her eyes were wide and blue, and her heart-shaped face was framed by a fringe of shiny blond hair. Greg could see her mounting disappointment; it was obvious that she'd really been looking forward to volunteering with the children today.

"Maybe I can help. I was just on my way up there. She could come with me and talk to Renee." To the girl, he added an aside. "Renee coordinates the children's volunteers."

The woman nodded hopefully, her smile brightening and widening to show a row of perfect, pearly teeth.

"Whatever," said Gina. The two of them started off toward the elevator.

"My name's Maggie," said the woman, extending her hand. Greg took it and shook. Her skin was soft, her short nails manicured a shell-like pink. "I really appreciate this. I've been looking forward to this for a long time. Kids mean a lot to me, ever since my brother…" Tears welled up in her blue eyes, and she looked away.

"My name's Greg," he said. "I'm happy to help." He didn't think that it would be wise or polite to pry about what had happened to her brother, so he let it go.

They reached the fourth floor and went to see Renee. "I

don't remember talking to you, but it's been such a busy week, who knows where my mind was. Grab a book from that shelf over there. We're always glad to have another volunteer."

For the rest of the hour, they, along with several other volunteers, read stories to the children. Greg normally spent this time trying to soak up all the good feelings in the room—the generosity of the volunteers who were so happy to donate their time, and the courage of these amazing children who were able to smile and laugh even in the midst of these bleak circumstances. But this morning, he got all of the good feeling that he needed from sneaking covert glances at Maggie. She seemed to embody the volunteer sprit. She read like a children's librarian, with great expression, throwing in funny voices for each of the characters. Her face lit up when the kids stopped her to ask questions or to laugh. If only everyone were just like her, thought Greg. I'd never be tempted to eat another human again.

The hour flew by. Maggie approached Greg, and they started toward the parking lot together. Greg liked the feeling of her walking beside him. He found himself dreading the moment when they'd split up to go to their respective vehicles.

"I had such a good time today," Maggie gushed. "Just seeing those kids smile like that. It was so rewarding."

"That's wonderful. I'm glad you enjoyed it. Will you be coming back next week?"

"I think so. How about you? How long have you been doing this?"

"Two years."

"What made you start?" she asked.

Greg didn't have many friends, due to his fear of killing them. He realized that no one had ever asked him this question before, and he didn't know what to say. "I guess you could say it was a personal tragedy that made me start. In a way, this helps me get past it. Maybe one day I can tell you more about it."

Maggie's eyes teared up again, and Greg guessed that she was thinking again of her brother. "It's the same with me. I'd like very much to talk about it, someday." They gave each other timid smiles, and Greg knew that this was going to be the start of something wonderful.

Without even meaning to, Greg passed his own car in the parking lot and kept walking with Maggie. She stopped when she reached her own car, a light blue Volvo station wagon. "Well, this is me," she said with a giggle.

"Oh, right. I'm sorry, I must have walked right passed my car. I was just…really enjoying talking to you." His stomach twisted in familiar knots. He knew that he was hungry, but tried to tell himself that it was just nerves.

"I had a really good time, too." Maggie smiled. And then, to Greg's astonishment, she leaned in to kiss him. Her face smelled sweet, like grapefruit, and a few strands of her blond hair tickled his skin. As her lips pressed against his, Greg involuntarily opened his mouth as if to bite down on her lip, but before he did, she backed away. Greg had never been so grateful for anything in his life.

"I'm sorry," said Maggie. She was blushing. "That was

so forward of me. I'm never like this. But it's strange. I just feel this…connection to you."

"Would you like to get some coffee?" he asked her.

—

They spent the rest of the day together. Coffee turned into lunch, which turned into a walk in the park, which turned into dinner. Greg had never felt so comfortable with anyone before, and by the time they were finishing dessert, he knew that he was falling in love. They talked about everything. Well, nearly everything. Of course, Greg had not gotten up the nerve to tell Maggie about his secret life as a vampire. Even so, he had hoped that for the first time, he'd found someone that it might be possible to share that awful secret with, someday.

After dinner, they decided to go for another walk, down by the lake in the park. The air was sweet and cool, and the moon shone bright overhead. Greg and Maggie sat down on a bench by the lake. Greg heard his stomach growling fiercely, and he ignored the pain with more ease than usual.

"I've had such a good time with you today," said Maggie.

"So have I. I really hope that we can do this again," said Greg, leaning in to kiss her.

And then things changed. As their heads leaned toward each other, Greg heard Maggie whisper, "But I don't think that will be possible." He saw the moonlight reflect of off one of Maggie's teeth. The teeth that had been so sweet and pearl-like earlier in the day, and were now elongated and sharp, just as his were in the seconds before feeding time.

Because he recognized what was happening, his reaction time was quicker than the normal person's would have been. He jumped up from the bench and yelled.

"What the…No! No, you can't be!"

Maggie was confused. How did Greg know what she was? How had he gotten away from her? She lunged after him, her arms flailing to catch hold of him. Greg grabbed her wrists and held them tight. Maggie strained against him, starving now, craning her neck in an effort to sink her teeth into him.

"Stop. Maggie. It won't do you any good. You see, I'm bloodless, too. Cut me if you like. You'll see. I'm one of you."

Maggie shook her head, shrinking back. The hunger ripped at her belly, and she stared at Greg hopelessly and disgustedly, as if he were a refrigerator holding nothing but a crusty bottle of mustard.

They sat back down on the bench. Maggie's teeth retracted. Neither of them spoke for quite a while.

Fortunately for Greg, he was too stunned to feel his heart breaking. How could this be? This beautiful, sweet girl, the one that he had hoped would help him reform his terrible urges, was a vampire too. How could she be reading to hospitalized children one minute, and trying to kill him the next?

"I don't understand. How do you do it? Don't you feel guilty? Doesn't it eat you up inside?"

"Why should it?" responded Maggie, examining her pink manicure in the moonlight.

"Because it's horrible, killing. Good people don't kill

other people. You're nothing but a hypocrite! You read to children, for God's sake!"

"Yes, I find it's a good place to pick up a victim. The men that read at hospitals, they tend to be so…gullible, so naïve. Don't you think?" She paused, then laughed. "Oh, of course you already know that. You were doing the same thing, weren't you?" She slapped him playfully on the arm. He recoiled in horror.

"I was not! I was there trying to inspire my better nature, trying to get over these unnatural urges."

"Unnatural? What do you mean? Oh, goodness. Surely you're not—"

"Not what?"

"Not one of them. An abstainer." She spat the word out disgustedly. Greg gave her a sheepish look. He'd never met another vampire before, except for the one that changed him. He hadn't realized that there were enough of them to be divided into subcultures.

"You ARE!" Maggie said with a laugh. "How quaint and old-fashioned. I didn't realize there were still any of you out there. How do you do it? Mice? Work at a slaughtering house?"

Now there was an idea. He'd never thought about a slaughtering house before…

Greg snapped out of it. Maggie was making fun of him. "Well, what am I supposed to do?"

She rolled her eyes. "You're a vampire, sweetie. You're supposed to be sustaining yourself through the drinking of human blood."

"I just can't. I was a vegetarian!"

Maggie laughed. She took his hand and her smile softened, moving to her eyes. "I do like you. I'm glad that I didn't have to kill you."

Greg laughed too. "Yeah, so am I." He squeezed her hand. His head was still swimming with the new information. He was horrified that Maggie had no problem eating humans, would have had no problem eating him if he'd turned out to be human. But that horror was far overshadowed by the comfort that he felt being next to Maggie. Finally, he'd met someone who could share his secret. Finally he'd met a woman that he wasn't afraid of harming in the night.

They sat for a while in comfortable silence. The moon overhead shimmered on the pond. "So, have you ever seen it work out for vampires like us? An abstainer and a…whatever you are?"

"A partaker."

"Of course."

"Who knows? I have a friend in a mixed marriage. It seems to work for her." Greg's heart felt light as he heard this information. They continued to sit on the bench for a long while, until Maggie's head drooped and rested on Greg's shoulder. As the sun's rays broke overhead, he whispered into her ear.

"Maggie, what do you say to breakfast? I've got a whole mess of rats that I've been fattening for weeks."

Maggie yawned and opened her eyes. "Hmmm" she said sleepily. I'll try anything once." They rose, and walked together to her car, still clasping hands.

ABOUT THE AUTHOR

Lydia Galt is an Alabama native who lives in Birmingham. She studied English in college and graduate school, and she enjoys reading, writing, cooking, and needlework.